THE FAIR AMERICAN

By ELIZABETH COATSWORTH

Dancing Tom

Alice-All-by-Herself

The Golden Horseshoe

Sword of the Wilderness

Cricket and the Emperor's Son

The Cat Who Went to Heaven

Knock at the Door

The Boy with the Parrot

The Sun's Diary

The Cat and the Captain

Toutou in Bondage

Away Goes Sally

Five Bushel Farm

The Fair American

The Fair American

THE
FAIR AMERICAN

BY

ELIZABETH COATSWORTH

PICTURES BY

HELEN SEWELL

NEW YORK

THE MACMILLAN COMPANY

1943

Set up and electrotyped. Published September, 1940.

Reprinted March, 1943.

PRINTED IN THE UNITED STATES OF AMERICA
AMERICAN BOOK—STRATFORD PRESS, INC., NEW YORK

To Aunt Anna Pardee,
who loves France and ships,
this story of France and a
ship is dedicated with much love.

CONTENTS

CHAPTER   PAGE

    I. ESCAPE   1

   II. AT THE HUNTING LODGE   11

  III. THE TAILOR'S BOY   19

  IV. ON THE ROAD   27

   V. THE ROYALISTS   38

  VI. THE CAPTAIN GOES ASHORE   47

 VII. THE NEW CABIN BOY   57

VIII. TROUBLE   65

  IX. ON BOARD THE FAIR AMERICAN   73

   X. THE DESERTER   82

  XI. THE GALE   94

 XII. WHO IS THIS BOY?   105

XIII. THE BIRD FLIES FREE   117

ILLUSTRATIONS

The Fair American   Frontispiece

Towers dark against the moon   7

Mad Marie with a crow on her shoulder   15

It was nearly dawn   25

A small furry face   31

A crying of sea gulls overhead   43

"I can't be ladylike when I'm so happy"   49

Stumbling a little sadly   63

Serene again   67

A little cage   86

Stretched miserably on the sofa   97

"Peter's the oldest"   113

Swung high into the air, basket and all   127

Upturned faces   131

THE FAIR AMERICAN

So long ago,
So far away—
There was sorrow then
As there is today.

There was danger then
And the troubled brow,
And kindness that flowered
As it does now.

There was courage too,
And the sea, and the land,
The quick warm heart
And the steady hand.

I

ESCAPE

THE FIRST THING that Pierre saw as he wakened was the moonlight that lay across the darkness of his room like the blade of some great sword. Jean, the old valet, was beside him, or at least the boy thought so; but since the man, whoever he was, carried no light, he could not be certain until he heard Jean's voice low and urgent:

"Get up, Master Pierre, quickly. They are coming back, I think."

Pierre slipped out of bed in silence. It was May, and the polished floor felt cold to his bare feet. He could smell the odor of damp earth and blossoming bushes from the overgrown gardens that surrounded the drafty old château in which he had always lived. He stood for a moment listening; but nothing stirred except something small in the ivy outside

1

his window, and near at hand the quick dry breathing of the servant.

"I hear nothing," said the boy.

"Hush." Again there came the whisper. "Here are your clothes. Hurry."

In the vague light Pierre dressed, feeling the practiced hands of Jean moving now at his knee adjusting a buckle, now touching his shoulder lightly to help him into his coat. Through all the haste he could feel the other listening; and now he, too, began to listen again, although it seemed to him he was too unhappy to care who came or on what errand. Yet he began to tremble a little.

"Where are the servants?" he asked, and again the old man said "Hush" and answered in his voice that seemed almost soundless.

"Gone, except Marthe. I hear her now."

There was a whisper of skirts and a deeper darkness in the door, and a smell of orris root across the smell of blossoms on the quiet air. Pierre saw Marthe's hands in the moonlight holding a white napkin filled, as he guessed, with food. She gave it to Jean. Now she began crying, too loudly for Jean's taste.

"We must be going," he told her. "Where did you see the torches moving?"

2

"Mostly along the road from the village," she answered, trying to control her tears; "a few around the stables. See, I found Madame's earrings hidden in the little drawer in the secretary. Everything else has been stolen by the others before they left."

She knelt down, kissing Pierre's hands. He felt her tears against them and tried to comfort her. She had been his mother's maid and, since Madame de la Tour's death, had stayed on as a sort of housekeeper. He remembered her face as far back as he could remember anything.

Jean pulled at his arm.

"Come! Come!" he whispered.

"Marthe must come too," Pierre said, but Jean snorted, "She'll be safe enough. It's her brother the blacksmith who will be leading the dogs."

"That is true," sobbed Marthe. "Go, while you have time. And may God protect you."

The house was old, and smelt of mold and damp stone, and soot in the chimneys. It was the only home Pierre had ever known, but it was too grim to love. Now it seemed menacing. The windows spied upon their flight. The stairs creaked, "Quick! Catch them! They are trying to get away from us!"

The bolt in the small door at the end of the passage stuck

3

and squealed, crying out to those who lay in wait outside. It seemed as though even stone and iron and wood hated their masters and had waited all these generations, like the peasants, to find a voice for their hatred. Pierre felt a kind of angry relief, as though he had escaped from some trap, when he followed Jean through the haunted door into the night.

"At least," he thought, "if they kill me here, it will be under the sky. Father died under the sky."

For a moment they stood, man and boy, a large shadow and a small shadow in the greater shadow of the house. Beyond them lay the clear undisturbed moonlight, as though a silver cloth had been spread on the lawn for a festival. Jean had planned his path. Holding the boy by the wrist, he sidled swiftly along the narrow shadow under the wall, and disappeared down a walk nearly blocked by its own overgrown hedges; for the garden, like much else at the château, had been long neglected.

A bird flew up and brought their breath back into their chests with a gulp. A mole scuttled underfoot. Now they could hear voices and catch the red smoky light of torches. Pierre wanted to ask why the men carried torches in moonlight, and then he answered his own question—"To burn the château when they have looted it."

Why were they so silent? he asked himself, and again he knew. The pillagers wished to catch the household unawares.

4

But why? Why should they wish to do him harm? He had grown up among them. He was not like his father, always at Court, always writing the agent for more and more rents to be sent to Paris. No, he had lived here in the village. He knew them all by name, had always known them.

Jean stopped suddenly, and Pierre collided against him and choked back an exclamation. Two men passed the entrance to their alley, and one lifted his torch; but the bushy young growth of the hedge shielded the fugitives, and the torch half blinded its holder.

"The birds haven't stirred," said his companion. "There's not been a candle moving in the château."

It was Jacques Bordon, Marthe's brother, who answered.

"That Jean is a sly one. We'll send him to the tribunal with the boy. He'll only be a good citizen when he's a dead one."

The other gave a snarl. "Why ask the tribunal to do our work?" he demanded. "We can kill our own game without calling in the tribunal."

"As you please," said Jacques Bordon. "I'm no spoilsport."

They passed on. Pierre in the shadows was less frightened than angered at hearing his fate so coolly decided upon. Jean's hand was gripping his until the bones hurt, one finger grinding against the next. Pierre could hear that the man's breathing had quickened, in an anger like his own. The valet

5

moved more boldly now. Their only hope was in moving quickly. He stooped for a branch and held it upright, and walked out into the moonlight of a drive. A man passed, with a torch.

"Curse!" muttered Jean as he went by the man. "My torch has gone out! We must find Bordon."

The man passed, his eyes on the château. The fugitives had gained another walk, raying out toward what had once been the deer park. When they had gone a hundred feet, Jean let go Pierre's hand and began to run. Pierre ran after him. It seemed to him that their flight was noisy, as they crashed and stumbled over winter deadwood; but by now the circle of men about the château was tightening, and all eyes were fixed upon its doors and lower windows. No one had time to notice a crackling in the underbrush, which, at any rate, would be but some wandering cow or sheep. No, they were after bigger game tonight—the master's son.

Jean reached the shelter of the deer park and turned. Here they were comparatively safe and might catch their breath, the leaves shielding them, the damp earth under their feet. The woods lay a little above the château, and, looking back, they could see it, with its tower, dark against the moon. The torches seemed pale, almost rosy, in the moon-whitened air. They formed a broken ring about the silent building.

6

Towers dark against the moon

As the two watched, they saw a group of men move toward the great door on the terrace. It was so still the heavy knocking came clearly to their ears.

The house remained silent.

Then Jacques Bordon's voice called loudly: "Open the door, you in there! Your neighbors have come to call!"

There was a coarse laugh from the crowd, but no stir nor sound came from the dark château.

A dozen torches were now grouped about the entrance, and, small and far off, the watchers could see the blacksmith doffing his liberty cap in a gesture of savage jest.

"Very well, citizens," came his voice in mock courtesy, "we will save you the trouble of opening the door."

Pierre caught his breath, seeing the man's arms swing back over his shoulder as the heavy blacksmith's hammer which he carried fell, splintering the oak of the door. The sound reached them after the sight, a loud reverberating crash, and at the sudden breaking of the silence there was an answering roar from the ring of peasants about the building.

Crash!

Shout!

Crash!

Shout!

The ugly music went on, till the dogs barked in the village and the women could be seen running across the dew-bright grass to join their men. Pierre did not love the house; he had always been lonely there, growing up with no mother and a father far away at Court. A little while ago he had felt as though the house hated him. But it was the home of his ancestors. It was terrible to see it attacked.

Jean reached out and touched him on the shoulder.

"Come away, Master Pierre," he said in a low voice. "It does no good for us to watch."

Blindly Pierre followed him, deeper and deeper into the woods, while behind them sounded one blow louder than all the rest, one final roar from the crowd; and then suddenly came a sort of humming silence as the mob was sucked into the house through its shattered door, and the trodden grass outside was left again to the moonlight.

9

The fields are spread like tablecloths
Which the Moon puts to dry,
And she has washed the high hilltops
And whitened all the sky.

Now pale, serene, and weary,
She glances round the night.
Is every flower silver?
Is each wild eyeball bright?

II

AT THE HUNTING LODGE

THE LITTLE HUNTING LODGE to which they came was damp and broken down. A heavy odor of rats and dust swept out to meet them as Jean forced open the door. Pierre hated to enter, in the darkness, but Jean was insistent.

"We must wait and see what will happen. It may be that the cooler heads in the village will interfere. I cannot believe that everyone is of this rogue Bordon's mind."

"May we not have a light?" Pierre asked. "Surely no one will come here. It has not been used for years, since my father was a young man."

"No," said Jean. "One cannot tell who may pass through the woods on a night like this."

"Then let us talk," said the boy. "I cannot sit here waiting and thinking."

"Talk low," replied the old man. "May I sit beside you? I am tired with all these events."

Pierre made room for Jean on the old rat-eaten blankets that the servant had found in a chest and spread neatly on a bench running along the wall facing the windows, through which they saw only darkness dotted by moonlight that shook as the leaves stirred in the breeze.

"My father," Pierre said, after a pause; "what had he done that they should have killed him in Paris, Jean?"

"He had the misfortune to be born a gentleman," said Jean grimly. "It seems it has become a crime in these days."

"But why do our people here hate him too, Jean? How they shouted this afternoon when word came of his death!"

The old valet was silent for a while.

"Your father," he said at last, gently, "was seldom on his estate, as you know, Master Pierre. He needed all the money he could get to keep up his position at Court. The agents here were often hard on the people in collecting the rents. No money went back into repairing the ditches, mending the roofs, or keeping up the stock. It all went to Paris. Still, it was perhaps not so much your father they hated. It is their own poverty and dirt and ignorance. Suddenly it seems to them the fault of the château, and all who belong to it."

The boy sat in silence, with the moonlight and the leaf-

12

shadows moving across his white face and unseeing eyes. He seemed to be thinking, and for a while there was silence except for the light scraping of a branch against the sagging roof.

"Jean," he asked at last, hesitantly, "was my father ashamed of me? I have often wondered."

The man gave a low exclamation of surprise.

"Ashamed?" he asked. "What curious ideas you keep shut up in your head, Master Pierre! Because he did not take you to Paris, or come here more often to see you? But that is the custom of the gentlemen. It cost all that the rents could bring to keep him at Court, and here naturally he was bored. When you had come of age you would have seen! Then he would have taken you with him everywhere."

"And we should have been friends," said the boy almost to himself. Suddenly he put his head on his companion's shoulder and sobbed, "I can never know him now."

"No," answered the old man in a voice that also shook with grief. "The old days are gone."

Again there was silence. Something ran across the roof. Something knocked against the pane, and brought their eyes back to the window.

"Look!" exclaimed Pierre. "What is that?"

Jean looked for a long time.

13

"They are burning the house," he said, and then cried out with sudden passion, "Oh! The scoundrels! The rogues!"

Pierre said nothing, but watched the column of smoke rolling and unrolling its great convolutions across the moonlit sky. Even where they sat they could hear the distant crackling of the flames; and a cock, wakened by the light, began crowing from some barnyard, a lovely triumphant sound which was caught up and answered from near and far.

Soon the fire, emboldened, shot up in tongues among the smoke, which now coiled like a dragon above its lair and now rose up in a revolving pillar, beautiful and terrible.

The two at the lodge had gained their feet and stood pressed in silence against the window, watching. The sight held them, unable to look away.

"There go the pigeons," murmured Jean. The birds were wheeling about in the sky, in and out of the smoke. There were hundreds of them, frightened from the great dovecot that stood near the barns. Perhaps someone had set a torch to it; for certainly the manor pigeons were hated, since they could not be killed when they flew down to eat the farmers' grain. Now they seemed a symbol of everything beautiful and long-protected, suddenly defenseless.

Jean glanced at the boy beside him. He should do something, he knew. This was no place now for his young master.

14

Mad Marie with a crow on her shoulder

But the events of the day had exhausted him. To escape from the château, to take shelter in the old lodge—so far he had been able to plan, thinking that surely something must happen to check this terrible forward-rush of events. But nothing had happened. He must do more and do it immediately, but in his exhaustion he could reach no decision.

"This isn't a St. John's Day Fire to be gaped at all evening," exclaimed a woman's voice behind them. "They'll be hunting for the boy soon. Jean Valet, you're a fool. The first place they'll come is here."

The two turned about with a start. They knew that wild tone. It was Mad Marie, who lived alone in the stone hut of the old pagans on the bare moors and wandered where she willed by day or by night, with a crow on her shoulder and the moor wind in her skirts. She had a terrifying way of running backward without stumbling, a knife in each hand, as fast as a man could run. Occasionally, when angered, she pursued someone, freezing him with terror. The boys herding cattle looked often over their shoulders, dreading her sudden passing. And even in the village the people crossed themselves when she came near and let her have whatever she chose to take, whether it was a loaf of bread cooling on a sill or an old dress drying on the grass.

Only the priest and Pierre were not afraid of her. Sometimes, riding on his pony, the boy had met her and stopped to talk with her. Once she had taken him to her den in the house of the ancients—more like a foxhole than a human habitation, but clean enough. It had a floor of fine gravel between the upright slabs of stone, under a roof of stone covered with earth, and there was a little fire on the hearth whose smoke trickled up among the roots of the furze overhead. Marie had given him blackberries that day picked from the hedges, of the kind the village people would never touch because they said a curse was on them, since from them the crown of thorns had been made. Their blackness was the mark of their guilt, the people thought; but Marie gave them to the boy in a wooden bowl, and poured over them cream from a jug that stood cooling in the shadows.

"The cows like my milking as well as any other," she said, looking at him with a grin. "He who has nothing has everything."

Pierre remembered that saying now.

"Fire, you have been a servant,
Kind and good,
Warming all within this household,
Baking food.
For two hundred years, and more too,
You have sung
Like a nurse beside the cradle
Of the young."

But the fire never hearkened,
Never stayed.
Up the shrinking walls its terrible
Path was made,
On the roof it leaped and capered,
Faster, faster,
Like a mad thing, laughing, panting—
"Now, I'm master!"

III

THE TAILOR'S BOY

I T WAS EASIER to see objects in the little hunting lodge. The cool broken pallor of the moon had been replaced by a smoky rose light, which wavered blindly up and down the rotting walls and shone on the woman's sardonic thin face.

"Still the little gentleman!" she exclaimed. "How do you expect to get him a mile along the roads like that, Jean Valet?"

Without waiting for an answer she took a bundle from her arm and brought from it a torn shirt, shapeless trousers, and worn shoes with wooden soles.

"Quick!" she said. "If they don't fit, all the better. No, don't shrink from the dirty cloth, my master. In dirt lies your only hope tonight."

When Jean had helped him to change, she tossed the man some peasant clothes for himself, while she brought out a

19

pair of dull scissors and began hacking and cutting at Pierre's hair, which fell to his shoulders. He permitted her to work without protest, but to himself he thought, "If I am to die, I would rather die as I was."

Still, he did not wish to die, and some quality in him of seeing things as they were recognized Marie's wisdom. Her next action, however, forced him to rebel. From her almost empty bundle she now brought forth a soiled white cloth and a jar filled with some salve whose coarse odor filled the room. This she smeared liberally on the cloth which she then began to wind about Pierre's neck.

"No, Marie," he said, starting back. "I should die with that dreadful smell always under my nose."

She grinned, and drew her forefinger about her neck in a sudden gesture.

"So, you'd like the knife better?" she asked, gibing at him. "See, Jean Valet, your young master gives himself away every time he speaks. Oh, the fine pretty talk of the gentlemen! It is like the music of birds! But if they hear this bird's music, they will wring his neck. Mine is the only plan. Your nephew is sick. He coughs so, he cannot speak. He can only whisper, poor lad, and even then the coughing wracks him."

Pierre, most unwillingly, allowed the dirty cloth to be

20

wound about his neck. The smell sickened him, but he would get used to it.

Marie handed the jar to Jean.

"Put it on every day fresh," she said. "The smell carries belief with it. Cough, my master; this masquerade is for your life. Show no disgust at anything. Disgust is the mark of your class. If you seem sick, it will explain your delicate looks, your fine hands. But go out, rub them in the dirt. Get it under your nails."

When Pierre came back from obeying her orders, Marie was still instructing Jean.

"You, too, are too fine to have been a farmer. Say that you were a tailor's man, you and the boy. Such long hours, and scarce enough pay to keep your backbone from piercing your belly! Then the citizens hung up the tailor at the lamp-post, and you are at last free. The boy's your nephew—the only kin you have since his father died of the cough. You want to get him to sea as a cabin boy in the hopes it may save him."

She shook Jean by the shoulders, her eyes staring deeply into his.

"You understand? With luck you may get him to Brest and aboard one of the American vessels. Be bold when you need be. Boldness will get you further than caution. Try to

21

get him to his uncle and aunt, the *émigrés*. They say they are in a port called Boston, somewhere on the seaboard."

Jean said, "I had forgotten about Madame de la Tour's brother, Monsieur le Baron. No word has come from him since he left at the beginning of the troubles."

"They say in the village he calls himself now Monsieur L'Étranger. Oh yes, he has written letters since he emigrated! The letters have not reached the château, but they have reached the schoolmaster and the village. They have reached Marie!"

She gave them a fierce scrutinizing look.

"Keep to the cattle trails along the moors tonight," she warned them. "Sleep all day. If you can find the standing stones of the old people, stay there. The villagers never go near them after dark, but they'll do you no more harm than any other stones. After two nights' travel you should be able to follow the roads, and may your wits guard you!"

With one last gesture she swept the napkin from Jean's hand and tumbled the food from it into her own dirty cloth.

"There," she said. "Take that. A monogrammed napkin might be death to you both. Now off on your ways, and I'll be off on mine."

But Pierre would not have her go so easily.

"If I live, it will be thanks to you and Jean," he told her

22

gravely. "Why have you been so good to me, Marie, when all the others have turned against me?"

"Because you were never afraid of me, child!" she said. "Hark! There is someone moving in the outskirts of the woods. But they'll move out again!" She gave a laugh that chilled her hearers' spines, and, catching two knives out of her belt, held them over her head and ran backward out of the door down the little path, a grotesque and terrifying figure.

Jean returned into the room and hastily flung the blanket into the chest. Then he ran outside and picked a branch, returned and swept out their footprints left in the dust. The meeting with Marie had aroused him and restored his courage. He had an objective once more, the port of Brest at the farthest point of Brittany, more than a hundred miles away. He had been given orders again; and, having lived all his life under orders, they were a help to him, even when given by Mad Marie.

"Come," he said to Pierre, "we must go as far as we can before dawn. The moon will be sinking soon"—and led the way upward through the trees toward the bare sweep of the moor beyond. The fire behind them still burned strongly, and with the veering wind they smelled the smoke of it and heard the shouts and the lowing of cattle and the startled

23

clucking of fowl as the villagers looted the barns. Once they heard, nearer them, a high shout of laughter like a fiend's, repeated three times, and a distant crashing in the underbrush that told where Marie was pursuing some intruder in the wood.

Out on the moor the sky seemed nearer and kinder again. They moved rapidly along the cattle paths, following westward, guided by the sinking moon. A hill rose between them and the burning house and the confusion about it, then another, and another. They were like dark wings screening the fugitives from the disaster behind them. The air was almost clear now from the smell of smoke. Sometimes they passed crags at the tops of the hills, and once a circle of stones, standing in a ring, where Druids perhaps had worshiped. Rabbits were hopping in the open places. The night dew wet the old clothes they wore, and the rough shoes Pierre had been given chafed his feet, but he kept on stubbornly. It was nearly dawn when at last he reached out and touched the valet's elbow.

"There is a cross on that hill," he said, with a grave smile. "Shall we sit there and eat something now . . . Uncle Jean?"

24

It was nearly dawn

The plant cut down to the root
Does not hate.
It uses all its strength
To grow once more.

Turn, boy, to the unknown field
Beyond the gate.
Never look back again
To the bolted door.

IV

ON THE ROAD

PIERRE AND JEAN rested that day in the shadow of a hill in a hollow among the furze, and the next night they traveled again. They had now come to country they did not know. It was more difficult for them to avoid the farmhouses, and several times they were forced to retreat before the fierce barking of the farm dogs. The food they had brought with them had been eaten. They had a handful of coppers, which Marie had tied up in her cloth, but nothing else except the earrings, which would be dangerous to show. Jean had fastened them in his hair which he wore clubbed at the neck and tied with black tape. If they should be searched, he trusted the jewels would not be found to condemn them. Boldness now was their only course. They must obey the mad woman's instructions and take to the road, trusting their wits.

27

On the second day they rested again in open country after their night wanderings. Below them they could see the post road, and about the middle of the morning they were awakened by the galloping of horses' hoofs, the creaking of harness, and the heavy rolling of wheels. It had not rained for several days, and the first thing they saw was the cloud of dust rising from some cavalcade and drifting slowly off into the moor. As the cloud approached, they could make out ten soldiers on horseback coming along at an easy canter, followed by a coach with three lead horses and two wheel horses, one mounted by the postilion, while another man cracked his long whip from the box. Ten more mounted soldiers followed in the dust of the wheels.

"It's the courier from Paris," said Jean. "They say that farther west the King's subjects are gathering. They must be in some large numbers for the courier to require such an escort."

Pierre stretched and felt his feet.

"How they ache!" he exclaimed. "The furze has scratched my legs too. Is there any food left, Uncle Jean?"

The man opened the cloth and brought out a dried slice of bread.

"There is this, Master Pierre."

"You must practice now saying Pierre, Uncle Jean. You

28

must speak to me roughly sometimes. Where is your own bread, Uncle?"

"I am not hungry," replied the man. His face looked pale and drawn.

Pierre divided the small slice.

"There is a bite for us each," he remarked. "No, take it, Uncle. We must feed our wits, for now it is time for us to follow the highway."

A change had taken place in the boy. At the time that word reached them of his father's death he had been but a child, looking to others for direction in any difficulty. But danger had brought out a new authority in him. Though he was sad enough at heart, he spoke with a sort of gaiety to the old man to keep up the other's courage.

Jean sighed and rose, tying the empty cloth to the stick he carried. In silence they walked down to the road through the last drifting dust of the courier's passing. It was easier walking here, bad as the road was. They no longer wasted their time zigzagging on uncertain paths, nor stumbling in great circles about the farms. At the next house they came to they stopped to buy a meal of broth and black bread, with a hunk of cheese. Here for the first time Jean told his story of the sick nephew whom he was taking to the sea, and here Pierre first coughed and whispered agreement.

29

"Poor lad," said the woman absent-mindedly. She had a teething baby in a box on the mud floor, and was boiling a pot of clothes in the caldron by the pigsty, and gave little thought to the travelers. Fortunately, too, she was somewhat deaf, for to a suspicious ear Jean's story would have seemed clumsily told, and Pierre's coughing not very convincing. Luckily for them the farmer's wife was in no mood for weighing their tale, but fed them and took their money, with her mind on other things.

Pierre and Jean went down the road with renewed courage. They had hot sustaining food in them at last, and they had appeared in their new roles and had been accepted for what they called themselves.

Next time they stopped to ask to sleep in a mow, it was with more assurance. For two days they traveled among scattered farms and small hamlets, but toward the evening of the second day they came to a town. On the outskirts they passed the ruins of a château, recently burned. The rosebushes about the blackened foundations were in full bloom, and a bird sat on a spray and sang as though the world had just been made and his was the first song ever sung.

Pierre stood listening, a dirty young figure, grotesque in his ill-fitting clothes and the evil-smelling linen about his thin neck. As he stood there, with Jean waiting wearily be-

A small furry face.

side him, there was a stir among the bushes and a small furry face peered out at them. Pierre whistled and a spaniel ran to him. It was pathetically thin and wild-looking. Some cuts and bruises on its side suggested that it had been stoned; but it showed no fear of the boy, though it growled when Jean tried to touch it.

"It must have belonged here," said the man. "It recognizes the gentry."

Carefully Pierre fed it with some scraps of bread and cheese from his pockets. Then he whistled to it to come with them. Jean spoke in alarm.

"It will be recognized and call attention to us. It is dangerous for us to have such a dog in our company."

"We can't leave it here to starve," answered Pierre. "Let us wait here then until it is dark, and skirt this town. After that we must take our chances."

The old man grumbled at the added risk, but in the end accepted it and helped Pierre disguise the little beast's all too evident air of gentility. They cut patches of hair from its side, trimmed its tail to the thinness of a rat's and muddied its face. It allowed Pierre to do anything he wished; and when all was done, even Jean admitted the animal would look a cur to any but the most experienced eye.

"Turk," Pierre called it, naming it for a dog his father

had brought him once from Paris, when he was a very little boy, the only gift he could now remember ever having been given him by that resplendent and aloof personage.

That night they skirted the town and returned to the highway on the other side. By now they acted their parts easily. When they came to the villages, Pierre hung on Jean's arm as though exhausted, and coughed bitterly while Jean wiped his face with the cloth and begged some kind-looking citizen or citizenness for food to help him to get his dying nephew to Brest. They had so little money left that now they begged where they could, nor were the people unkind to them.

In every square monuments had been set up, engraved "Liberty, Equality and Brotherhood—or Death," and the townspeople all wore the tricolor cockade of the Republic, and said "citizen" and "citizenness" with every breath. There were no priests on the street and the churches were filled with painted scenery like theaters, where orators proclaimed the virtues of the Republic from the old pulpits.

Once they passed an inn just as a woman was coming out, wearing a little white feather in her bonnet. At first no one seemed to notice it; then a market woman called out something, and a crowd gathered, threatening the first woman, who looked terrified and began to weep. Suddenly she tore off the bonnet and stepped on it.

"It was a mistake!" she cried. "I had forgotten that white was the royal color. Will someone give me a cockade?"

A rough-looking man handed her his, and she, picking up her broken headgear, tore out the offending feather and pinned the cockade in its place. The crowd cheered, the woman gave a trembling smile, and the incident was over.

"She was lucky," said Jean in a low voice. He had stood with his hand on Pierre's elbow holding him back. Both of them were shaking with excitement. It was in the next town that they themselves walked into danger.

The place seemed like any other of the small, rather prosperous villages of central Brittany, and, like the others, it was held by the government and its atmosphere was Republican. They had gone to the small inn on the square, as it was noonday, and the landlady, a fat good-natured woman, had given them each a bowl of rye bread and milk gone a little sour. There were several men drinking at a table, and one of these, a small youngish man, with an eye that looked askew, began to question Jean as he leaned back in his chair. His companions went on drinking and paid small attention to him; but Jean and Pierre were soon aware that he was suspicious of them and was amusing himself, leaning back with crossed knees, asking Jean now this and now that about his past life and his plans, speaking gently to Pierre, and

34

now and then stopping to laugh soundlessly. While this was going on, and Pierre could feel the rising panic beating at his breast as he forced himself to swallow one choking spoonful after another, the day's courier dashed up amid the escort of soldiers, and the man who had been pestering them rose with a final careless glance, stretched, paid his bill, and went out.

"He is going to inform on us!" whispered Pierre.

Jean nodded, a blind look of helplessness in his eyes.

Pierre jumped to his feet. The words of Mad Marie rang in his ears. "Boldness will get you further than caution."

He walked out to the officer of the escort and began pleading with him to take them with him on the next relay.

"They say there are royalists in the woods," he whispered hoarsely. "My uncle and I are afraid. We are very light. The horses would never notice us if we each rode behind a soldier. Or we could ride in the coach. Have pity on us!" And he burst into a mingled paroxysm of tears and coughing. He was acting, and acting now for his life.

"Have pity on us, brave captain," he croaked again, reaching out his dirty hands to touch the officer's sleeve.

"It's against the regulations!" said the officer, not unkindly. "The royalists are not after such as you and your uncle."

"Please, citizen! We are afraid!" moaned Pierre, and

35

this time the officer drove him off more roughly. But Pierre knelt on the cobbles beseeching him.

The harried soldier turned to Jean.

"Take your nephew away!" he ordered him. "Or I shall use my whip." And with that he strode into the inn. The informer followed, and tried to speak to him in the doorway.

"Nonsense!" they heard the officer shout. "I have talked with them myself. You've been drinking and are ready to call the fleas that bite you royalists!"

"Shall we go now?" asked Jean, barely moving his lips.

"Not till the courier leaves," answered Pierre in the same way.

When the officer came out, wiping the wine from his mouth, to mount the fresh horse that had been brought him, the boy again pressed forward with his prayer and had to be pulled out of the way of the horse's hoofs by his uncle. The soldier gave him a half-pitying gesture of farewell, as he galloped off, and straightway forgot him. Boldness had succeeded.

As the echoes of the hoofs died away, Pierre and Jean, followed by Turk, took once more to the road.

He who has never known hunger
Has never known how good
The taste of bread may be,
The kindliness of food.

V

THE ROYALISTS

Westward the land grew poorer, the farms smaller, the towns less frequent, and the forests and wild lands wider and more embracing. Here the people were taciturn and suspicious. There were still the Republican officers in each village, and the tablets to the Republic stood in the squares; but fewer people wore the cockade, and candles burned on the altars of the little moss-encrusted stone churches.

Men were unwilling to talk, not knowing whether their neighbors were friends or enemies; but Pierre and Jean began to hear tales of the royalists living in the forest, harrying now here, now there, burning one night the farm of some well-known Republican and on the next night, thirty miles away, rousing some judge of the new tribunals from his bed to give him his own justice.

The deeds they heard of were fierce and cruel. Though

these men were fighting for his cause, Pierre had no desire to share in their vengeances.

At one town they were told that the local small garrison of soldiers had been informed of a gathering of the royalists near by and had ridden off to try to capture the leaders. While they were gone, the Paris courier drove in. His escort of soldiers refused to go farther.

"But the other escort is not here," he protested.

"That is not our affair," replied the officer. "We have obeyed our orders in coming with you so far. We were told to return immediately."

"But it is death for a courier not to go on!" cried the man, wringing his hands.

"That is your affair, citizen. You will have to take your chances with the brigands," replied the soldier coolly.

The new relay of horses was harnessed to the coach, and, white-faced, the courier, with only his postilion, drove off westward.

Following on foot some hours later, Pierre and Jean came upon pieces of paper blowing about in a lonely spot where the road passed through the beechwoods. It was late afternoon, and already under the trees dusk had come and the blowing papers seemed bleached like bones.

"That is odd," said Pierre uneasily.

39

Turk ran ahead of them, and came back, barking, with his tail between his legs.

Now they could see the overturned coach by the side of the road. The courier was lying dead a little beyond, and the postilion among the trees, as though he had tried to escape. Four of the horses, too, were dead, shot down to stop the coach. The fifth had probably been ridden off by the royalists, for the harness had been cut.

Pierre knelt with Jean beside him and said a prayer for the souls of this unknown man and boy. They were their enemies, true; but they were French too, and had died as Pierre and Jean might die at any hour in these violent times. Probably they were as innocent of any hatred or ill-doing as the two who prayed for them on the rutted road. Only the chance of birth had decided to which party they should belong.

The woods grew thicker, and no clearing came, no human being passed them. Turk kept so close to Pierre's heels that often the boy's shoes struck him by mistake; but still he crowded close, looking over his shoulders fearfully toward the shadows under the beeches. The humans felt the same mood of suspense and terror, and it came almost as a relief to hear at last a motion in the underbrush and to find themselves surrounded by a group of men.

"Who are you and what is your business on the King's road?" demanded a burly man whose face was half hidden under a broad hat.

Pierre motioned to Jean to untie the cloth about his neck. When the hated ugliness was gone he answered clearly, "I am Monsieur Pierre de la Tour, son of François de la Tour of Quidec. My father died by the guillotine three weeks ago in Paris, and with the aid of Jean here, my servant, I escaped when the house at Quidec was burned. We are trying to get to Brest on the chance that we may succeed in emigrating on some neutral vessel."

There was no mistaking Pierre's voice or manner. The men about him dropped their threatening air, and soon led him with Jean to join the main body of royalists in the woods at supper. There seemed to be thirty or forty men of all ages and kinds—gentlemen, servants, and peasants—under the command of a passionate white-faced old man who had not formed part of the group on the highway. While they ate roasted venison, he tried to urge Pierre to join with his forces.

"Even a young boy can do something to avenge a father!" he cried. "See, I am old, but I have a daughter and two sons whose blood cries out to me from the ground day and night."

He seemed half maddened by grief. His servant told Jean

41

later that the old man never slept. There was something terrible and pathetic about him. When Pierre refused to join his followers, he called the boy an unnatural son and a coward.

Pierre looked at him quietly.

"If I could meet the men who condemned my father, I should do my best to kill them," he said. "But it would not ease my sorrow to help in the destroying of some postilion or farmer whom I had never seen before, and who had done me no harm."

"Vengeance strikes where it may!" cried the old man vehemently, but the next morning when Pierre and Jean were starting off early he suddenly appeared.

"Here," said he to Jean, "is food for your master on the way." Then he turned to Pierre.

"My son," he went on, "I spoke harshly last night. Forgive me. Often I scarcely know what I am saying. It may be that my way is wrong and that yours is right. If grief can give a blessing, mine goes with you."

Two of the royalists accompanied them to the edge of the forest, five miles on their way. They told them many stories of their companions, and by what tragic routes they had come into hiding.

"We do not have much time to remember," said one man,

42

A crying of sea gulls overhead

with a grim laugh. "Our remembrance speaks with bullets and the sword."

Pierre was glad to bid them farewell. The shadows of the beeches, for all their young summer green of leaves and dapplings of light, seemed a place of horror and hate. Having lived so much alone with his thoughts, the boy saw life in his own way. There seemed to him right and wrong on both sides of this struggle. He was not called upon to judge between them. It was enough if he could escape.

After the forest they came to moorland and gorse again, and here there was a crying of sea gulls overhead, and a distant brightening of the sky which spoke of the sea beyond the sight, like a mirror reflecting its light back upon the haze of the horizon. It was now June. They had been on the road for nearly two weeks, and their feet were hardened, and their faces had lost the first look of exhaustion. They had passed through so much danger that they were growing a little careless of it. Even Turk felt the lightening of anxiety and ran along the ditches in a quivering search for rabbits.

Pierre found himself humming tuneless little songs. This danger, this hardship, this excitement made him feel alive as he had never felt, moping about in the echoing rooms of the château, wondering how he might employ his time to pass the many hours that stretched before him each day and must be lived through somehow.

Jean looked at him sometimes secretly, and nodded his head with satisfaction. This was a son of whom the master would have approved. The boy had lost his indoor pallor and languid way of moving. It would be hard to pretend at Brest that he was dying of the cough. Still they must be on their guard. Brest was in the hands of the Republicans. They would be watching the port for refugees; and it would be hard, indeed, if they should be caught at the last moment, after all they had gone through to escape.

"Come, Master Pierre," the old man said one morning. "I have put Marie's salve again on the cloth. You must get back to your coughing, for today we should reach Brest."

To have nothing at all
Is to have much still:
One's share in the sun,
And the winds that blow,
A right in the road
That swings over the hill,
And the far horizon
That lies below.

To have nothing at all
Does not take from the mind
Its free roving thoughts
Which still know their abode,
Nor the hope that's ahead,
Nor the sorrow behind,
Nor the future that lies
At the turn of the road.

VI

THE CAPTAIN GOES ASHORE

THE MORNING WAS FINE, the tide was right, and the *Fair American* had all her cargo in the hold and was ready to weigh anchor for home; but the papers which the port officials had promised had not arrived.

"They love to show their power by keeping everyone dangling at their office doors," snorted Captain Patterson, striding up and down the deck in a fine temper. "I'd like to run for it; but we'd be fired upon by the forts, and I can't risk that with you along, Deborah."

His wife looked up at him from her chair, smiling above the sewing in her lap. She was making him a fine shirt, with a high French stock that would come up to his ears in the latest fashion. Mrs. Deborah was a little shy, even with her husband.

"I like it here with all the masts in the harbor and the

47

bells from the town," she said, "but I do hope they'll not keep you if you desire to go, Captain Patterson."

The captain patted her shoulder absent-mindedly.

"This is your first foreign port, Debby," he told her. "If you had seen as many as I have— Well, I'll go ashore and find out what may be done to stir things up. After the cargo's aboard, every day we linger adds to the expenses of the voyage. Will you come with me, my dear?"

She shook her head.

"I like to watch the town from here," she murmured. "With such terrible things going on everywhere, I don't desire to go too near."

"Then I'll take the children," Captain Patterson said. "Sally!" he added in a shout. "Andrew! Look lively if you're going ashore with me!" And to his wife he added in a lower tone, "They will be perfectly safe, my dear, and there is nothing distressing to be seen on the streets. It's as though I were to take them down Batterymarch Street in Boston."

There was a galloping race of feet from somewhere forward, and the children appeared, out of breath, and caught Captain Patterson each by a hand in a babble of excited questions.

"Hush," cautioned Mrs. Deborah, leaning over to pat the

48

"I can't be ladylike when I'm so happy"

little girl's shoulder. "Sally, child, be quiet, like Andrew. It is more seemly for a young female."

But her eyes had their gentle smiling look, as Sally impetuously turned and flung her arms about her aunt's neck.

"Oh, Aunt Debby," she gasped, "I *can't* be ladylike when I'm so happy. Andrew and I have been wishing and wishing and wishing all month to go up into the town—and now we're really *going!*" And she kissed her aunt out of pure happiness.

"Quickly then, Sally! Get ready," said the captain, his hand on his son's shoulder. It was a curious thing this, he thought, sailing with a wife and children aboard, but the Yankee skippers often did it. It was good to have one's home with one, and Andrew, his motherless son, under his eye again, and Debby with him as his wife, and to know that it was she who had been so good to the boy when everyone had thought the *Fair American* and her captain were at the bottom of the sea. As for his wife's niece, Sally, she was like a kitten on board, taking prettiness and playfulness with her wherever she went. It had not been easy to get her Aunt Nannie to agree that she might go, even on a summer voyage, even though the captain swore on his honor there was no danger by land or sea.

50

But Sally had finally coaxed permission, with the backing of Uncle Joseph and Uncle Eben.

"I'll be with Aunt Debby," she argued, "and Andrew will take care of me too—and, of course, Uncle John. And Dinah desires it *so* much!"

So, in the end, Sally, too, had come—with Dinah, the black cat, and Brindle, to be ship's cow and live in the long boat with the pigs and chickens. Eunice, her doll, had come too.

Sally admitted later that Eunice was not a good sailor after all, and preferred to be left most of the time propped against the pillow in her berth.

It had been the merriest voyage that Captain Patterson could ever recall having taken, and on the whole the children had not been in the way. They deserved a reward now that the business of selling the cargo and reloading was over. They should see the sights of a foreign port, or at least a few of them.

"Pray don't ever let go their hands, Captain Patterson," Mrs. Deborah called as she waved the ship's boat good-by from the deck.

"Good-by! Good-by!" called back the captain and the children. The days were warm, and Captain Patterson had rigged up an awning over part of the deck by the cabin.

51

While in port Mrs. Debby's chair stood in its shadow, with her sewing table at hand and near by a little flowering rose tree in a pot which her husband had brought back from Brest on the first day.

"There, my love," he had said, "is a small garden for you. But I can't promise that we'll get it safely home. The fresh water may well become too precious to use for flowers."

Standing beside the roses in her white sprigged dress, with black Dinah at her feet, Mrs. Deborah waved and blew them a kiss. Sally, waving back, suddenly realized that her aunt's pose had an anxious look. She cupped her hands on either side of her mouth, and hallooed, "We'll be careful, Aunt Debby."

Her voice echoed over the hot transparent harbor water, among the sea gulls, past the high hulls of anchored ships, away, away toward the breakwater and the sea beyond.

Did Aunt Debby hear? They could see her kerchief waving against the shadow under the awning. The boat moved forward, smoothly, with the short chop of the oars in the oar locks and the swing of disturbed reflections behind them.

Now the boat was nosing along the stone quay toward the green slippery stairs that led up from the water. The sailors steadied it with their hands while the children stepped out, carefully throwing their balance so as not to slip on the seaweed of steps that half the day were under water. Looking up, Sally was a little frightened by the faces that stared down at her from above—dark, fierce, changing faces, with straggling hair and dirty tricolor cockades in what was left of their hats. It was a comfort to slip her hand into her uncle's and, pressing a little against his side, to step through the crowd of idlers who had watched them disembark.

No one tried to stop them. She heard the unintelligible talk of a foreign language and could not make out a word of it, though she had studied French with Aunt Debby and Andrew on the voyage over. But these men spoke so much faster than Aunt Debby had ever spoken, with her lesson book open on her knee; these men spoke so much more vehemently than Aunt Debby ever spoke that Sally was bewildered. It was as though she had stepped into a land of savages; and although the people whom they met later on the narrow cobbled streets seemed more like the villagers she knew at home in Maine, something of her first dread remained, like a shadow over the bright day.

But Captain Patterson walked easily along, whistling, a child's hand in each of his. Now and then he pointed out something to them, the ruins of a town house that the crowd had sacked and fired, or a monument at the corner of a street erected to the Republic. But his mind was on what he was planning to say at the office of the harbor master. His broad shoulders were squared, his clean-shaven chin was up, and there was a stubborn light in his blue eyes.

Recognizing the signs, the children trotted along quietly, now and then saying something to each other in low voices so as not to disturb the captain's thoughts. Sally's brown eyes and Andrew's gray-blue ones missed little. They saw the market women, with their baskets, and the rough country carts bringing their produce in from the farms. Some of the soldiers they passed were barefoot, but they carried themselves proudly in their ill-fitting uniforms. The blinds in the houses were all closed; but the children sometimes saw them move a little, as though someone inside were looking out at them. The roofs were steep and slated, with high dormer windows where a few plants stood in pots.

In spite of the laughter and shouts that came to them from the open doors of the wineshops, there was an air of sadness about the town. Its cats were thin, and its doors needed paint. Sally was glad that Aunt Debby had stayed on the *Fair American*.

The office of the harbor master was large and hot, and flies crawled aimlessly up the windowpanes and fell weakly down onto the sill once more. One pane had been broken and stuffed with what looked to be a striped shirt. The clerks, in their untidy wigs, seemed as aimless and buzzing as the flies. Only the harbor master was terribly neat, a small man, tight-looking all over, who seemed unwilling to waste even his glances and most of the time sat looking down at the nails of his left hand, which he held crossed over his right, as though warning it against any impulsive action. To all the vehement things Captain Patterson had to say through the interpreter, he only replied with an almost imperceptible shrug, or the barest opening of the mouth. The children felt as though they were facing a stone, so little response did the man make. It came almost as a shock when, at the end of Captain Patterson's address, the harbor master picked up a paper, signed it without flourish, and handed it to the American with a mere, "There, citizen captain."

He did not appear to hear Captain Patterson's thanks, nor notice Sally's curtsy and Andrew's bow. His eyes were once more absorbed in the study of his own hands, held before him on the table. Captain Patterson, looking at him, cut short his thanks and, marshaling the children before him, left the office briskly.

"There!" he exclaimed at the door, in high good humor. "Now, thanks to our grudging friend in there, our troubles are over."

A harbor is a doorway,
A harbor is a shop.
There the ships who go to market
Often stop.

There the ships who go to market
Stop to buy.
"I'll have some of this, and this, please,
This I'll try.

"I have sold what I brought with me.
I can pay.
Well, good-by—perhaps you'll see me
Back, someday."

VII

THE NEW CABIN BOY

I<small>T WAS AS THEY STOOD</small> on the steps above the street that
Sally saw the old man and the boy with the cloth about his
throat and the little dog. She could not have said why she
especially noticed them. Perhaps it was because of something
different about them, or perhaps it was because of the fixed
way in which they were looking at the captain and Andrew
and herself; but she knew immediately that these strangers
wanted to speak to them, and were afraid.

She smiled and nodded reassuringly, tugging at Captain
Patterson's sleeve.

"Uncle," she said, "those people over there have something to ask you."

"Beggars," replied Captain Patterson, glancing at them
carelessly. "The town is full of beggars." But because he had
succeeded in procuring his permission to leave the harbor

and was in high good humor, he drew a coin from his pocket.

"There, Andrew," he said. "Take it over to those people at the corner. We can help someone, anyhow."

Andrew, walking gravely toward the other boy, the coin held out, saw him draw back almost as from a blow. But the old man spoke to him sharply, and the French boy took the money, his face flushing quickly and then turning pale under the brown. Andrew suddenly thought of a race horse, at once so proud and high-strung. Were beggars like this? he wondered.

But the man, murmuring something, had drawn the boy toward Captain Patterson and was speaking to him earnestly, pointing at his companion. The American stood there, good-natured and handsome.

"Yes, yes, you keep the money!" he smiled, rocking forward onto his toes and back. "Glad for you to have it." But as the old man kept on with his insistent eager words, the captain began to look impatient. He drew another coin from his pocket.

"There, citizen!" he said, handing it to the old man. "Now the children and I must be going." And as the other tried to detain him, he pushed past with a warning "Enough's enough, my man."

58

Sally, almost on tiptoe, her mouth a little open, had been listening. It seemed as though she had been listening with all her being, with her eyes, her ears, and her very mouth— as though her heart had been listening.

"Uncle John," she cried, following him. "They're in trouble. I think he was saying, 'Please take him with you. He is the last one left.' He said it so often I began to understand. Uncle John, please don't go so fast. It wasn't money they wanted. They wanted you to take the boy on the *Fair American*."

Captain Patterson had regained his good humor.

"What a little goose you are, Sally," he said, taking her hand again. "I can't take all the boys of France along with us just because they ask. Let them pocket the louis and be satisfied."

Sally pulled her hand free and faced Captain Patterson.

"He's only a little older than Andrew, Uncle John," she remarked gravely. "Suppose it *was* Andrew and he was in trouble." A sudden pain went through Captain Patterson's heart. Andrew *had* been in trouble, a lost child, not knowing if he had a relative in the world; and, out of the indifference of fate, Sally's aunt and Sally had been sent to rescue him. He looked at Andrew, who looked back confidingly, sure that his father would do the thing that was to be done. He felt

59

Sally's impatient, pleading hands pulling at his sleeve, trying to turn him.

"I'll see about this," he muttered, a little threateningly, in his quarter-deck manner, as he turned back toward the group he had just left.

"Now," he said sternly to the old man. "Speak up! What's this all about?"

Again the man tried to tell him, speaking low, repeating his phrases, silent when anyone passed. Again the boy stood, tense and anxious, with the same look of self-control about his lips and dark eyes that asked no favors. Again the little dog retreated against his master's briar-torn legs. This time Captain Patterson, accustomed to judge men, really studied the faces before him, and found out from them more than the two children could make out from the words that were said.

He frowned a little, pinching his lips, while the others waited anxiously. He saw that there might be danger involved, and he had Sally and Andrew with him. He ought to run no risks. But, on the other hand, he could not determine to abandon the French boy, now that he had had a good look at him.

"Well, something must be left to chance," he thought, squaring his shoulders. He nodded to the old man.

60

"Very well," he said, and put his hand on the boy's shoulder. "I'll sign him on as cabin boy."

Tears rushed to the Frenchman's eyes—tears of relief, that he quickly brushed aside, afraid to show so much emotion in a public place. The boy drew a quivering breath and turned pale again, while Sally hopped up and down silently clapping her hands, her curls bobbing under her bonnet, and Andrew said, "Oh, thank you, sir," in a low voice.

The captain felt he might as well be hanged for a sheep as a lamb. He pointed to the old man and then toward the harbor, and raised his brows questioningly. Did he, too, wish to go? But the other shook his head. His thanks poured out, and his explanations. Sally, quicker than Andrew to understand this new tongue, though slower to speak it, interpreted, "He says something, Uncle John, about going back to his old village."

"I venture he'll be safe enough, once he gets rid of this boy," the captain said. "He looks like anyone else. But the boy, now, you couldn't hide the breeding back of him from anyone who took the trouble to look."

The good-bys were quickly over. The boy seemed almost stunned by losing his last touch with his old life. As for his companion, relief and sorrow struggled on his face. Bending down, with a sudden gesture, he touched the boy's hand

61

with his lips, slipped a small parcel in the child's unheeding grasp, and, turning, walked rapidly away without a backward glance.

"Jean!" called the boy after him. "Jean!" He started to follow, but Captain Patterson touched his shoulder again and shook his head.

"No," he said. "Come along with us." And the boy, understanding the tone if not the words, fell into step behind his new friends, his heavy shoes stumbling a little sadly over the cobbles.

Stumbling a little sadly

Shall we sail for China,
Or shall we sail for Spain,
Or shall we try the harbors
Of Africa again?

Shall we purchase spices,
Or shall we carry teas?
Or Russian hides and iron
To bring across the seas?

What will they buy in Boston,
Or need in Baltimore?
What present shall I bring my wife
She's never seen before?

VIII

TROUBLE

IT WAS NOT UNTIL they were on the quays that they met
with any trouble. No one on the streets had given them more
than a passing glance, especially after Captain Patterson had
taken the precaution of stopping a market woman, and buy-
ing a basket of cheeses for the new cabin boy to carry. Except
for his wild look of torn clothes and straggling elflocks, he
might have been any little servant following his foreign
master, in the eyes of the townspeople, each busy about his
own affairs.

But on the docks the idlers had no affairs of their own.
They sat in the sun, on bales or pierheads, spitting into the
water, scratching their matted heads under the liberty caps
they wore.

It was an old one-eyed sailor who heaved himself slowly

to his feet and swaggered over toward the man and the three children, followed by one or two others.

The captain saw him coming but neither slowed nor quickened his step, even when the man stopped in his path and, jerking his thumb at the boy, said something which was clearly a question as to who he was and where they might be taking him.

"No parlez-vous," the captain snorted, bearing down at the other. He had dropped the children's hands and now walked a little ahead of them, truculently, his small convoy close at his heels. But the raised voices had gathered a crowd of loafers, always eager for a fight and now made more savage by the scenes they had taken part in during these months of revolution.

The stairs were still somewhat ahead, and the ship's boat lay out of sight at its foot. Captain Patterson saw no sign of the two sailors he had left in charge. They were probably asleep in the thwarts. He considered shouting to them, but knew that to call for help was a sign of weakness, likely to bring on trouble in a rush. His best chance lay in an air of cold indifference, while he got as near to the stairs as he could.

But now there were men behind him as well as in front, and someone had laid his hands on the French boy's shoulders and spun him roughly round. Captain Patterson heard

66

Serene again

Sally's "Don't you dare touch him—he's ours!" and then the smack of Andrew's small fist, and a roar of teasing laughter. He turned, his own fists doubled; but just then another man appeared on the scene, a tall thin figure with a long nose and a pair of squinting gray eyes, and cocked-up shoulders squeezed into a uniform. This man had boots on and epaulettes, and a sword trailed at his lean side. He appeared to be an officer; but the remarkable thing was that he spoke in English, mixed with a torrent of French—the French addressed to the crowd, which drew back, and the English to Captain Patterson, whom he seized by the hand, shaking it violently.

"Oh, sir!" he exclaimed. "I am proud to meet an American, a citizen of that other Republic for which I also fought. The world has known one great man, a noble human being and a valiant soldier—George Washington!"

Still shaking the captain's hand, he whipped off his hat with its cockade and held it at his breast with his head bowed, as though in prayer.

"George Washington," he repeated, taking Captain Patterson familiarly by the arm. "I saw him often, for I served under Lafayette. A perfect man, citizen. It was an honor to tread the same earth."

The crowd had fallen back; but the leader began snarling

68

some protest in the ear of the officer, who glanced back at the French boy.

"My cabin boy," explained Captain Patterson.

"Of course," said the officer affably. "Nothing more natural."

Then he turned a face suddenly galvanized with fury at the one-eyed man and his companions, and poured forth a torrent of abuse upon them, ending with a savage gesture of a finger across the throat. The crowd melted away—even the leader, surly still.

"Ah," continued the officer, serene again. "They don't like to be reminded that their own necks may come under the guillotine too. General Washington was fortunate in having no such dogs to handle."

Talking of America, he sauntered to the head of the steps and shook hands with the captain for a last time. The sailors below had sprung to their positions and were steadying the boat. As the children passed down the stairs, now shortened by high tide, the officer gave the French boy one appraising glance, shrugged, and said, with a smile, to Captain Patterson, "The great Washington never made war on children. I wish you all a good voyage to America"—and, with a rather sad look on his long face, saluted and walked away.

One of the sailors took the basket of cheeses and helped

the new cabin boy into the bow of the boat, for he seemed
rather bewildered. The little dog leaped hastily over the
gunwale after him and scrambled to his side. The sailor
looked questioningly at the captain, who nodded to let the
beast be and then stepped into the stern with the other children. The men pushed off with their oars; the boat swayed
a little, balanced, and settled down to the short swing of the
strokes; and the stone quays, and the stone houses and
towers behind them, dropped slowly farther and farther
behind.

Suddenly Captain Patterson gave a short, amused laugh.

"What are you thinking of, sir?" asked Sally, leaning
against his shoulder.

"I was just thinking, child," said the captain, "that I had
promised myself to bring your aunt a present at parting from
France, and I think, after all, we have one here much to her
liking."

To stretch, asleep,
On the deck in the sun,
Or to doze
In a sail that's furled,
And at night
To make the gray rats run—
That's the way
To see the world!
If you're a cat
Of spirit and sense,
That's the way
To see the world!

The waves lie far
Below the rail;
The galley door
Lies near.
There's always a shadow
From the sail
If the sun shines
Too hot and clear.
For a cat who knows
His way about
The good things
Always lie near.

The smell of new ports
Where a cat can rove
And the sights are strange
As may be.

What tales I shall have
To tell by the stove
When I am too old
For the sea!
For a cat who retires
When whiskers turn gray
Should bring back
Fine tales from the sea!

IX

ON BOARD THE *FAIR AMERICAN*

THAT DAY, WITH THE EBBING of the tide, the *Fair Ameri-can* weighed anchor and headed out for sea, followed by a billowing convoy of gulls. It was late afternoon, and it seemed beautiful to see the yellow sunlight paint the sails again, and to hear the ordered cries of the sailors, and to feel the vessel lift again to the long swell beneath her bows. There was a figurehead at the bowsprit, carved like a woman with her hands outstretched and her white draperies apparently wind-blown back against her. Her eyes had an unseeing look, and there was a crown, painted with stars, in the wooden curls of her hair. She was, the children knew, the *Fair American* herself, the spirit of the ship; and they often watched her on fine days, leaning over the rail.

"See," said Andrew, "she looks different. She is glad to

73

be away after a whole month at port. She's glad to be at sea and going home."

"So am I," agreed Sally. "How good it smells, doesn't it? And hear the waves against the ship again! It reminds me just a little of the oxen at night, feeding in the darkness of the barn. There's a stamping and a rustling too—though, of course, it's not *really* much the same."

"But I know what you mean," said Andrew. "And the gulls might be the cats at milking time."

Just then Dinah passed them, but she would not come at their call. She had a preoccupied look, and kept stopping to test the air in a dissatisfied way.

"She smells little Turk," laughed Sally.

By now they knew that the boy's name was Pierre—Pierre L'Étranger, he called himself—Pierre the Stranger—and his dog was Turk.

"I wish Mother would finish with Pierre," said Andrew, with still that little air of shy pleasure which it gave him, even after all these months, to call his Miss Debby "Mother."

But when Pierre at last came up on deck they scarcely recognized him. He was dressed in an old suit of Andrew's, too small for him, showing his long fine wrists and making him seem even thinner than he was. But how he carried himself, what an air there was to him even in his awkwardness, added to by a landsman's ignorance of how to walk the deck at sea. The cloth was gone from his neck, the dirt from his skin; and Mrs. Deborah had washed and combed out, as well as she could, his hair in waves that covered the hacking of Marie's scissors.

She took her charge to Captain Patterson. "My love, here's your cabin boy," she said, looking pleased.

The captain's eye swept him.

"Humph," he admitted, "a real transformation, Debby, on my word. But don't throw away his old things yet. France is behind us"—he gestured toward the rocky bare coast and the stony town, already pale along the skyline—"but we may meet with a French frigate yet. Tom!" he shouted, and when the negro cook thrust his grinning head from the galley door, he added, "Take this boy and make him useful," and turned his attention to studying the sails.

Mrs. Deborah looked a little disappointed; and so did Sally and Andrew, hurrying up to join Pierre on the quarter-deck, only to find him gone. "You haven't stood your own watch," added Captain Patterson, not looking down. "Off to the longboat with you!"

It was the children's duty to feed and water Brindle, and the chickens who lived with the pigs in a sort of sty in the longboat. Nantucket Bob, who had been a whaler, cleaned

75

the stall and sty and fed the pigs. He said that, after being on a whaling ship and used to the smell of a dead whale, a pig seemed like a rose. Bob usually did the milking too; but sometimes the children took a turn at that, now that Brindle had her sea legs and was not so restless as she had been at first.

There were two new French pigs, leaning in a corner of their sty, braced against the motion of the ship, looking at the children from small suspicious eyes. Sally and Andrew stopped to scratch their backs for them with a stick they kept handy for scratching pigs' backs.

"They grunt differently," said Andrew. "They say *oui*, *oui*. Listen! Curly won't look at them."

Curly was the last of the American pigs, the one with a tail curled extra-tight. The others had disappeared one by one into the pot, and the children had sighed and accepted the fate of pigs. But they had the captain's own promise that Brindle should go ashore at Bangor with the rest of the family, and return to Five Bushel Farm with great stories of her adventures to tell the other cows on the long winter evenings when the snow lay deep beyond the walls.

Mr. Abel Bliss, the psalm-singing mate, passed them.

"Jump lively, there," he ordered, and the children answered, "Aye, aye, sir"—and scuttled off for the galley, where the grain was kept. They found Pierre on a bench just outside the galley door, peeling potatoes neatly and swiftly, in spite of the unaccustomed motion of the brig.

"That boy am sure quick to learn," said Tom, grinning at them.

"Tom, show Pierre the wound you got when the Indian tried to shoot your master," Sally begged, and Tom, grinning wider than ever, opened his shirt on the great scarred black expanse of his chest. The children loved the story of Tom and his master in Savannah, and of how the Indian had been angry with the white man for coming to shoot on tribal land, and had leveled his gun at him where he sat in his canoe. Tom had been paddling and had thrown himself sideways to shield his master. He had been in bed for six months, near death, and when he recovered, his master gave him his freedom.

"So Ah cum off to sea," ended Tom, as always. "Maybe someday Ah see Africy. But Ah ain't never spied it yet."

The mate's shadow passed like a hawk's, and the children took their pan of chicken feed and, with a shy grin at Pierre, departed along the tilting deck.

Sally, a few minutes later, listening to the cluck and clatter of the hens, thought of home and of Aunt Nannie feeding the hens at the kitchen door of Five Bushel Farm. The thrushes would be singing from the pines beyond the clearing, or was it too late for the thrushes? Sally was not sure, but she heard the clear unhurried sweetness of it in her mind. The Uncles and Jehoshaphat Mountain would have finished cutting the hay. It should be a wonderful crop, on new land, and there would still be corn growing, with its tasseled ears, among the blackened stumps of the last clearing.

She wondered what Hannibal, the bear, was doing in the forest and whether he ever remembered that he had been a pet cub once upon a time. Now that they were turned toward home, she was suddenly eager to be there again, with Aunt Nannie and Uncle Joseph and jolly Uncle Eben, and to visit Aunt Esther just up the river. Uncle John would, of course, be off on the *Fair American* most of the time, but Aunt Debby and Andrew would be at the farm for the winter. As for Pierre, she wondered.

"It's my turn to milk," said Andrew, who had learned to milk at the farm and liked to show his skill.

Sally nodded, and he reached under the longboat and brought out the three-legged stool they used and the pattens they always wore when they went into the stall. Sally handed him the scoured pail, that flashed now in the sunset. Brindle stood patiently, as he milked, her legs a little apart, braced against the swaying of the vessel. Once she looked kindly over her shoulder, her mouth filled with hay. She was not

78

a pretty cow, with her uneven horns and her coat like a striped cat's; but she was the gentlest cow at Five Bushel Farm, and that was why she had been chosen to be ship's cow and cross the sea.

Jon, the Swede, passed them, grinning, to take his trick at the wheel. Mr. Bliss, the mate, had been particular to make sure he was not a Finn—for Finns brought bad luck to a ship, he said. Mr. Bliss was very religious, but he was very superstitious too. In calm weather Andrew had found him sticking a knife into the mainmast to make it call up a breeze; and when almost immediately a breeze came, he took it out again, with a look at the mast which seemed to say, "You see what you get when you encourage calm weather when I'm around."

Sally, leaning against the side of the longboat—her hair stirred by the breeze, now this way, now that; her nostrils filled with the ship smell of tar and sailcloth and salt air; her body moving with a kind of joy to the leap of the vessel, eager under her feet—heard now, nearer than the straining of the cordage and the slap and hiss of water, the sound of a step beside her.

It was Pierre, with the pail of new peelings in his hand which he emptied into the trough. Relieved of its weight, he stretched himself and looked about him—at the immensity of the sea; at the last faint line of land, like a row of more stationary waves; at the sails against the streaming cloud rack of sunset. He had lost his dazed look and seemed like the sails themselves, thrumming with eagerness. Then his glance met the other child's.

"Sally," he said tentatively; and when she smiled, he smiled back at her, almost gaily.

This air that blows in from the sea
No one has breathed before
Save only porpoises as they play
In waves far out from shore,
Or whales whose tranquil breathings rise
In fountains of white spray,
Or sailors leaning on the rails
Of ships from far away.

Sea gulls with nostrils of strong bone
Have tasted this keen breeze,
And gannets in their billowing flight,
But nothing less than these—
Nothing save creatures strong and wild,
As vigorous and free,
Themselves, as is the wind that blows
So coldly from the sea.

X

THE DESERTER

Pierre had never known the sea. It was a new world to him, with its endless horizons and its great skies above the toss and tumble of the waves. He had known nothing like a ship, making her way mysteriously across these surging wastes, sometimes fleeing before the wind and sometimes stubbornly tacking back and forth, back and forth, forcing her way forward almost into the eye of the wind itself. He had never known the quick exhilaration of sea air, the damp push against his body, the bright sparkle along the upraised slant of the billows, the phosphorous creaming at the bows at night. He had never before slept to the cradling of the sea, feeling himself rocked between billow and billow, with the splash and gurgle of water in his ears mixed with the hum of cordage and the sudden flap of sails or the running of feet overhead. It seemed as though he had been born a new person after all the sorrow and horror he had learned on land; and because nothing he saw reminded him of his old life, he found his memory of it growing dim and far away, and his real existence came to be about him.

Life on board ship was rough and ready, and a quick blow that knocked a man headlong into the scuppers was considered the best cure for any carelessness or stupidity. But everyone was patient with Pierre, and he was quick and eager to learn, though at first, in his ignorance, he made many mistakes; and, of course, it was harder for him, speaking only French. Mrs. Deborah saw this.

"May I have Pierre in the afternoons when the children have their lessons, Captain Patterson?" she asked her husband on the day of sailing, when the boy was serving his first meal to the family and mates at the long mahogany table in the captain's cabin.

"Certainly, my love," the captain agreed.

It was Mrs. Deborah who, by little gestures, helped Pierre through the ordeal of that first meal, indicating without speaking where things should be placed, and where he should stand, and when it was time for him to go back to the galley. Captain Patterson was absolute ruler of the *Fair American*, except in the cabin, which was Mrs. Deborah's kingdom on stormy days, or in her little corner of the quarter-deck where in fine weather she sat, gently throned in a little cushioned chair with the children about her and Dinah asleep in the sun on the white scrubbed deck.

The best time of the day for Pierre was the hour he spent near her with Sally and Andrew. Mrs. Deborah would point to an object, Pierre would name it in French, one of the other children would name it in English, and amid much laughter and repeated efforts they would each try to pronounce the word in the other's language. Pierre was a good teacher, and Mrs. Deborah, who had found little profit herself in the lessons she had read out to the children on the voyage over to France, began to join the others in repeating words after Pierre and in trying out short phrases at his direction. Sometimes Captain Patterson would stroll up for a minute and lean on the back of his wife's chair, smiling and listening to them, before some slight shift in the feel of the planks under his feet, some vibration of the wall of sails towering above them, would send him on to give new orders.

The only warring note was struck by Turk and Dinah, who were for a while very suspicious of each other, Turk at first sitting against Pierre's knee, uttering low protesting growls or exasperated barks, while Dinah glared balefully down at him from the cabin roof.

"Aren't you ashamed, Dinah?" Sally scolded. "Turk's your guest, and you're behaving most ungenteelly! Why don't you say 'Bon jour, mon petit chien' nicely, you bad black cat?"

Dinah, having expressed her disapproval, soon settled down. She had adjusted herself even to bear cubs in her time. This little dog, scarcely larger than she was herself, was not worth the energy of a real feud; and soon they were lapping milk from the same dish, though Dinah still slapped out a lightning paw if she felt herself being crowded.

It was on the third day out from harbor that the little land bird lighted in the rigging. How it came to have been blown so far, whither it had been flying with its desperate small wings, no one could imagine. In all that wide immensity of water only the *Fair American*, like a small island of wood and leaning towers of canvas, could offer it any shelter; and there it clung, exhausted, watching them all with its round bright eyes.

A sailor went toward it and almost put his hand on it before the poor bird fluttered away onto the deck. Others closed about it.

"Oh, have a care!" cried Mrs. Deborah, troubled. "You'll force it off the ship!"

Pierre, hearing her voice, ran forward and neatly caught

85

the bird under his handkerchief and brought it to her. It was a great wonder to the children to see it in her hands, not fluttering, not even seeming afraid. The ship's carpenter was called upon to make it a little cage, and meantime Mrs. Deborah kept it in her work basket with a temporary top.

A little cage

The crumbs they brought, the little thing would not touch; but at last when Sally thought of the chicken feed, it pecked a few grains and delighted them by uttering a single cheep.

"Now," said Mrs. Deborah, "will one of you bring a saucer of fresh water? We'll put the basket well out of Dinah's reach and let Dick rest."

The bird was not the only excitement that they met with in these early days of the voyage. The next day the *Fair American* was almost becalmed. There were clouds in the sky which scarcely stirred at all, because the breeze was so slight. A slow swell moved on the sea, so that the brig rolled in a leisurely fashion, with barely headway enough to give her life. Every sail was spread—mainsails, topsails, and jibs—but the canvas often slatted in a sudden dead calm, and it took all Captain Patterson's skill to keep his vessel under way at all. The air itself had something listless about it, and everyone moved with dragging feet.

The chief interest to the children was in the great ship that lay ahead, off the lee rail, as becalmed as themselves. They had passed other sails on the horizon, but this was the first vessel that had been at all close to them.

"She's not a frigate," said Captain Patterson, looking at her closely through his glass. "I'm glad too. The less we see of frigates, British or French, the better for us. Now that they're at war, they neither of them respect the rights of neutrals. The British might take us for a prize because we've been trading in a French port, and a French frigate would be just as likely to claim we'd stopped in England in spite of our papers. You can't tell what captain you'll fall in with. It all depends on that, these days."

He stopped and then added, with a smile, "But it's the chance of being taken and sold as a prize that makes the profits so high. We Yankees love to fish in troubled waters."

"If she's not a frigate," asked Sally, "what may she be?"

"I take it she's a British East Indiaman, child," said the captain. "If she were American, I'd hail her and go aboard to exchange news. But I'm not overfond of an Englishman, particularly one in the Calcutta trade."

Sally looked her question; and Captain Patterson frowned, his eyes on his memories.

"It's a long and dangerous voyage," he went on, "and there are ugly tales of what goes on in some of those ships. But there's no doubt they make a handsome show, though the *Fair American* is a faster sailer."

All morning the children kept an eye on the approaching vessel, moving toward them as slowly as a cloud. By noon it was clear that they would pass very close to each other. The children could see now the officers on the other's quarter-deck and the sailors in the rigging. She was coming on with the waves, not across them like the *Fair American,* and the motion made her seem to be executing a series of slow curtsies as she advanced. Just as Pierre announced dinner in the cabin the American vessel passed by the big Indiaman's lion figurehead and slowly drew away, so near that the staring children could see the faces of the English crew looking back at them. Suddenly there was a movement by the rail, and the flash of a figure leaping far out into the sea from the other deck.

"Oh!" cried Sally, covering her eyes. "A man's jumped overboard!"

Andrew moved beside her, his shoulder against hers. Pierre stared at the water where the man had gone down. Now his quick eye caught the head and outflung arm of a swimmer some distance away, swimming the open ocean toward the *Fair American*. Captain Patterson was shouting to lower the boat. From the Indiaman could be heard whistles, and men running and crowding.

"Lower away, boys, cheerily now. Beat the Britishers to it!" exhorted Mr. Bliss.

The boat struck the water; and before it had stopped rocking with the impact, it was manned, with Mr. Bliss at the stern, and heading out toward the sailor in the water.

The Indiaman was a little slower in getting off a boat; but while the Americans, leaning over the gunwale, were hauling in the swimmer, the English boat was being manned and coming upon the scene.

89

"Here, you! Keep away from that man! We'll take him up!" shouted the brisk young officer at the bow.

"You'll have to get him first," called back Mr. Bliss, his usually solemn face lighted with the joy of battle.

Pierre stood at the rail, his hands clenched tight. He knew what it was to be a fugitive. With all his heart he longed for the escape of this unknown man.

"By what right do you steal one of our men?" shouted the young Englishman.

His boat was coming up after Mr. Bliss, but not able to overtake him. The *Fair American* had not slackened her slow headway. With every minute she was drawing a little farther away from the Indiaman; and though her own boat was overhauling her, the British boat, with each stroke, was drawing farther and farther from the protection of its mother ship.

The officer realized this and gave an order, and his men rested on their oars.

"By what right do you take that man?" he shouted again, indignantly.

"He says he's an American," yelled back Mr. Bliss.

They had reached the *Fair American* now and the waiting ladder dangling along the side.

90

"It's a lie!" shouted the officer, unheeded, as they climbed aboard.

Pierre never forgot the first glimpse he had of Dan Forrest, naked to the waist, his back laced with scars, his hair dripping across the devil-may-care light in his eyes, as the mate led him forward to the captain.

Behind them the other boat was rowing back to the Indiaman, which had shifted her course.

"Well," said Captain Patterson, "you're an American, are you? Where were you born, then?"

The sailor pulled his forelock.

"In Boston, sir," said he. The drip made a slow puddle around his bare feet.

"Boston, England, or Boston, Massachusetts?" demanded the captain. It was hard to tell what he was thinking or what he meant to do.

"Massachusetts, sir," replied the man.

"Ah, then," said Captain Patterson slowly, "what's the weather vane on Faneuil Hall?"

There was a silence in which the nearest sound was the drip-drop of water that fell down from the edges of the man's trousers to the deck.

"It's a ship, sir," guessed the sailor.

"You're a liar!" answered the captain. "You've never seen

91

Boston in your life. You're British, and I've no rights to be meddling with you. But British or not, I won't hand you back to them and the treatment you'd get. If you do your work here, you'll have no reason to complain."

He paused, and then added with a fierceness the children had never heard before from his lips, "But if I find, my man, that you're a troublemaker, I'll feed you on shavings and sawdust."

"Aye, aye, sir," said the man, pulling his forelock again.

Pierre drew a deep sigh of relief when he saw the sailor following Mr. Bliss toward the fo'castle, where the men slept and kept their sea chests. He had understood only some of the words, but it was clear that the fugitive was to stay aboard. "So much cruelty in the world!" he thought. "So many men escaping from the hands of their fellows!"

Mrs. Deborah touched her husband's sleeve.

"I'm so glad," she said simply. "Will they try to overtake us?"

The captain glanced carelessly behind him.

"They'll try, perhaps," he said, "but they won't succeed. I've been watching her all morning and she's not fast. With the boat to pick up, she'll soon see that she's wasting her time with us. Boy, didn't you say dinner was on the table?"

The hawk was not so terrible
As this sea.
Where may I perch
To rest my weariness?
There is not any rock
Nor any tree—
Only this sky,
This tossing dreariness.
I am so little
I can fly no more.
My hope is gone.
There is no other shore.

XI

THE GALE

FARTHER AND FARTHER sailed the *Fair American* out into the Middle Atlantic. Dick recovered and would even sing for his mistress. Curly, in his turn, disappeared from the longboat, and there were fewer chickens now for Sally to feed. Turk and Dinah suddenly became friends. It was a common sight to see them walking down the deck shoulder to shoulder, or curled up asleep together in a corner out of the wind.

One day Nantucket Bob showed the children the spoutings of two whales.

"It's exactly like the fountain we had in the garden," thought Pierre.

But these were living fountains indeed, breathed out by great animals. Bob told them about the different kinds of whales.

"No, they ain't fish," he explained. "Who ever heard of fish nursing their calves? But I've seen an old cow whale doing it many a time. And she'd be as proud and careful of her baby as anyone. And the bull whale—he's a fighting father! Tries to look after the family same as a man. Many a time I've thought it was a pity to go barging in on the poor things, harpooning them and the like."

By now Pierre could understand nearly everything he was told, if only it were said slowly. When he didn't understand, he would turn to Sally, who would explain in mixed English and French that often ended in gales of laughter.

Once they hailed the ship *Orion* from Newport; and Captain Patterson went aboard and came back with newspapers a month old, which he read carefully—especially the items on the sailing of ships and the prices of commodities. Every voyage was a gamble: one not only staked one's luck against storms and the chances of a world at war, but against a market which might recently have received several shipments of the very cargo one was bringing. To be first home with some new and desirable merchandise was the dream of every captain, and Captain Patterson, pulling his ear thoughtfully as he read the items, looked satisfied.

"We should make a very pretty thing of this voyage, Debby," he said to his wife. "You bring luck with you."

"I think the luck must come from the rose tree you brought me," she replied. "See how it keeps on blooming even in the cabin, and lashed into the corner there! It likes the sea as much as I do."

And it was true that quiet, timid Mrs. Deborah was never sick at sea, and never afraid, not even during the awful hours of the gale which they soon ran into. They had crossed without meeting with any rough weather; but on the return voyage, toward the end of the fifth week, when they were beginning to talk about home, the *Fair American* ran into a storm. The barometer dropped; and the wind began blowing very hard, driving a dark rack of clouds before it that seemed so close that they pressed down upon the sea itself, which rose against them in a kind of insistent fury. The sails were all double-reefed; but the sea was on the beam, and a great deal of water was shipped. The *Fair American* groaned and tossed. Her bow, striking down into the trough of a wave, jarred the entire hull, which seemed, half-buried, to shudder and lie still before it began painfully to climb the next wave.

Sally, stretched miserably on the mahogany sofa in the cabin, was not at first afraid. She thought of the figurehead, dripping with spray, battling against the seas, leading the vessel to safety; but after a while she was not so sure of the

Stretched miserably on the sofa

Fair American. It was better to open her eyes and fix their dizzy gaze on Aunt Debby, quietly sewing near by, her sewing basket tied to a leg of the table and her chair wedged between its edge and the wall. Aunt Debby would never look so calm, she thought, if they were all going to die.

Andrew, who had been kneeling with his face to the port-hole, came back to say that the clouds were nearly black now and the waves were washing over the deck without breaking. Sally, always so brave on land, began to cry, without sound, though no one would have heard her above the howling of the wind, the cataract sound of the waves, the rumble of the pumps, and the groaning of the ship mixed with all the sharp crash of sliding dishes and overturned furniture.

Captain Patterson came into the cabin, his face wet and quiet.

"All's fine," he remarked cheerfully. "How do you like life at sea, Andy boy? Debby, the wind should moderate at sunset." And then his comforting presence was gone again.

But the wind did not moderate at sunset, and the captain ordered a third reef in the mainsail. All night the *Fair American* tossed and struggled. No one went to bed at all; food was swallowed cold, as no fire could be kept in the galley stove. Pierre, who had been nearly as sick as Sally, found his sea legs and made himself useful. Poor Turk was shut into

98

the galley cupboard to keep him from rolling. Unlike Dinah, who retired, on her own paws, to Sally's bunk for an uneasy nap, he could not keep his footing.

Suddenly, just as the helm was relieved, a tremendous crash was heard.

"What was that?" Sally shrieked, jumping up from the sofa.

"The foremast must have gone," cried Andrew, starting out on deck; but Aunt Debby caught him by the shoulder.

"Wait until your father tells us what to do," she said steadily.

Pierre and Black Tom came and stood beside her, their eyes on her face. They could hear feet running overhead, shouts, and another loud splintering at the bow. The vessel had come up into the wind.

"That's the bowsprit now. She won't obey the helm," explained Andrew, and his face was very pale. He sat down beside Sally, who was being nearly thrown off the sofa by the violent motion of the ship. "Father will know what to do," he kept saying, trying to reassure her, trying to hold her steady.

The *Fair American* was rolling terribly now; and there was a heavy thumping against her side, where the spars that had fallen overboard were striking against her.

99

"She'll break open!" cried Sally, burying her head in Andrew's shoulder. "Oh, I *am* so afraid."

"You weren't afraid of the Indians," said Andy, in lulls of the uproar.

"They were just *people!*" cried poor Sally.

It was terrible waiting in the ill-lighted cabin, tilted now this way, now that, thrown against each other, not knowing what was happening outside, not able to do anything but wait—wait either for the ship to roll over at last or for something to be done to help in this extremity.

They heard a shout above them, another rush of feet, and then a pause—a human pause, at least, for there was no pause in the attack of the sea upon the brig, which was now wallowing helplessly under the blows of her own foremast and spars alongside. Then again the feet passed, this time more orderly.

"Praise be!" said Black Tom. "They's got the foremast cut away."

Gradually the blows against the side of the vessel lessened, and they knew the spars, too, had been cut free and allowed to drift astern.

At dawn Captain Patterson came in again, walking a little blindly.

"All right, Debby," he said wearily. "We've got her cut

clear of the wreckage and the wind's going down and we'll soon rig a jury mast. It's all right now, but it was close for a while."

"Close?" asked Mrs. Debby gently.

"The stay had to be cut," he went on. "It runs from the head of the mainmast to the head of the foremast. With the foremast overboard the stay had the whole weight of it, held half out of the water, and the mainmast was ready to snap under the strain. Someone had to go to the mainmast head to cut it, and the shrouds, Debby, were going slack and then bringing up with a terrible jerk with every roll. I wasn't sure a man could climb the shrouds tonight, Debby."

"Who did?" asked Mrs. Deborah.

"It was Dan Forrest, the Englishman, who volunteered. He got halfway up," said the captain. "Then one of those jerks tore his hold loose. I thought it was all over with us when I saw him fall. But he fell into the mainsail. It was lowered part way down, and it caught him like a cradle. He wasn't hurt."

Captain Patterson paused and passed his hand quickly across his eyes.

"The second time he tried, he got to the mainmast head. I don't now know how he did it, shaken as he must have been by the fall. With the stay cut, the ship was free from the wreckage. You must have felt the difference down here. The rest was easy—by comparison."

"Can't you rest now, my dearest?" asked Mrs. Debby.

But the captain gave a short laugh. "I'll turn in tonight," he said. "We have the jury mast to rig now and the wreckage to save. But you and the children should rest. You can stick in your berths now. . . . Ah, good boy," he added, for Pierre had brought him a mug of cold coffee, rich with cream, and corn bread—in his hand, since he could not come on any unbroken plate in his hurry.

When he was gone, Mrs. Deborah and the children went to bed. A wet wild light was coming through the portholes; and though the ship was still rolling violently, it seemed nothing to the earlier paroxysms they had known. Even Sally, still dizzy and bewildered, slept from plain exhaustion, and either heard or dreamed she heard the voice of Mr. Abel Bliss singing a loud hymn of praise for their deliverance, whose words drifted away, mixed with the howling of the wind. But Captain Patterson did not go to bed when the jury mast had been rigged and the brig once more answered to her helm in the quieting sea.

It was just as he gave a last look about him at mainsail and jury sail, at the still littered deck and the unshaven crew,

102

that his glance, by habit, swung outward to the sky and the sea beyond.

"What is that sail, mister?" he asked the mate sharply.

"I believe she's a frigate, sir," Mr. Bliss replied. "I've noticed her for the last hour, and I believe she's following us."

The storm snapped its fingers—
"Ship, are you afraid?
Now's the time, my pretty one,
To show how you were made!

"Were your timbers seasoned,
Built of chosen wood?
And your sheathing honest?
And your canvas good?

"Did the men who made you
Build with careful thought?
Dream each line and ponder
When your hull was wrought?"

The storm rent sky and ocean—
"Ship, are you afraid?
Now's the time, my little bird,
To prove how you were made!"

XII

WHO IS THIS BOY?

WHEN MRS. DEBORAH came on deck with Sally late that morning, she was instantly aware that something new was in the air. She looked about her. The soaking decks sent forth a cold sea smell and the *Fair American* had a battered look, with part of the rail gone where the foremast had crashed through it, and water-darkened sailcloth, and spars lashed near the fo'castle.

But the sails were all spread, and the ship, while moving more awkwardly under her improvised rigging, was bowling along with a stiff breeze. The crew, though haggard, were working steadily, putting things to rights; but she noticed that they glanced often aft, and Mr. Bliss, passing her with a bow and a "Good morning, ma'am," had been singing a hymn under his breath—always, with him, a sign of trouble, but whether over or to come she was not quite sure.

"See, Aunt Debby, the rainbow," said Sally. The child looked thinner than she had. Her eyes were too big, and her curls, for once, hung damply on her shoulders; but already Mrs. Deborah noticed that the fresh air on deck was doing her good.

Mrs. Deborah looked about for the rainbow, over miles of sliding, rather oily-looking sea. They were in sunshine, but far off there was a blown column of rain; and there, almost directly in their wake, she saw the full radiant arch of a rainbow, touching the sea on each side, with a ship sailing straight through it as though through some magic gate. Porpoises were playing in the waves near them, curvetting into view and then rolling out of sight again with a wild gaiety that quickened her breath to watch.

"Child," she murmured softly, the color coming into her face with pleasure, "it is almost worth the storm to see the ocean like this."

Andrew ran up to say that five of the chickens had been lost overboard, and that Brindle had broken the tip of one of her horns during the gale. The children chattered as usual; but still Mrs. Deborah could not put from her spirit a sense of oppression, of coming danger. She saw her husband studying the other vessel through his glass, and then talking with the mate, frowning.

"He looks the way he will look when he is an old man," she thought. She wanted to ask him what the trouble was, but held herself back. He would tell her when it was time for her to know.

She saw Zekiel Daniels, the bos'n, go aft, and caught his words.

"The men are afraid she's British, sir. They don't want anything to happen to Dan Forrest, not after his climbing to the mainmast head."

"You tell them if any man is taken off this vessel I'll follow him round the world till I get him back," replied Captain Patterson, speaking loudly.

She saw the bos'n take off his sailor's hat and bow.

"The men will thank you, sir," he said gratefully, going forward again.

She saw the captain's eye on the sails. Soon the mate was giving orders to bend a topsail on the jury mast, but there was an ominous creaking of the wood that made the captain order it down again. The *Fair American* was crippled. Her best speed was not enough. Even Mrs. Deborah could see that the ship, which she had thought so beautiful, was drawing up on them; and now it seemed terrible to her as some white monster, though she didn't yet understand why she should be afraid.

107

"You don't hear what we say to you, Aunt Debby," Sally complained at her elbow. "Why do you keep looking back at that sail?"

"I don't know, child," said Mrs. Deborah. "Because everyone else does, I suppose."

"Is it chasing us?" asked Sally suddenly. "I do believe it is!" And before her aunt could stop her, she had flashed off to the quarter-deck.

"Uncle John," she begged, pulling at his sleeve, "is that ship chasing us?"

"It would seem so, Sally," said Captain Patterson, a little grimly.

"But she can't catch the *Fair American!*" boasted Sally.

"I'm afraid she can," said the captain, "with our foremast gone anyway. But we'll see. A stern chase is a long chase. We'll wait and see what happens. Now, run back to your aunt, child."

It was a horrible day. No one could do anything except hold all sail possible. The mate ordered the second watch below to rest; but they straggled back, one by one, to study the oncoming sail behind them.

There was a grim fascination to it that kept drawing everyone's eyes from his occupation. A rain shower passed; and the carpenter brought sweet water to Mrs. Deborah, which he had caught in a fold of sailcloth for her rose tree. Dan Forrest practiced a Yankee twang amid some laughter, but the laughter was uneasy.

Mrs. Deborah, listening but asking no questions, gathered that most of the men thought the vessel behind them was an English frigate. A few thought she might be French, cruising for prizes from Santo Domingo. In either case the *Fair American* was neutral and should not be disturbed; but Mrs. Deborah gathered that some captains on both sides had little scruple in taking American vessels as prizes, pretending to find some irregularity in their papers.

Noontime came and went and then slow afternoon, with its varnish of bright warm light. The rain had drifted away, and the sky was nearly cloudless. They could clearly see the hull of the pursuing vessel now, and the gun ports; but she showed no flag to tell her nationality. Captain Patterson had gone below and shaved and put on his new uniform. Mrs. Deborah dressed the children and herself fresh and combed their hair, breeze-ruffled. The long-dreaded moment had arrived. At about four o'clock they heard a hail, but kept on.

A puff of white, a loud detonation, and a cannon shot fell into the sea off their bows, splashing the deck with water. Captain Patterson shouted, the *Fair American* hove to, and the bos'n ran up the American flag. Sally, standing excitedly beside Andy, felt a sudden leap of her heart as she saw its brightness take the wind. The frigate had broken out its own flag—the heavy bars of the new French Republic—and come up also into the wind.

"They won't take Dan Forrest then," said someone.

"She may be British for all that," muttered Captain Patterson; but by now they could see the Latin faces crowding the rail, and hear the shouts of *"Bonne prise! Bonne prise!"*

"You'd think we were at war to hear the scoundrels!" exclaimed Mr. Bliss indignantly. "Oh, if we had only a few guns to teach them their manners!"

An officer now hailed them in English, ordering the captain to come aboard with his papers.

"Come aboard yourself," Captain Patterson hailed back.

Pierre was standing with the other children, beside them, yet apart from them. These were people of his own race, with only a narrow strip of water between them. He felt a sudden yearning toward them, and then a kind of dread. They were of his race, but the killers of his father. He would not have much to hope for from their hands.

A boat had been manned and was crossing to the *Fair American*. The crew gazed curiously at the officer as he came aboard. He was young, and wore his uniform rather awkwardly. The four French sailors remained at the oars, fending off from the side of the vessel with every wave.

Captain Patterson came forward and bowed, introducing himself.

"What ship is this?" the Frenchman asked in careful English.

"The *Fair American* from Providence."

"How long has she had that name?" the other went on, with a kind of sneer.

"We never have but one name to *our* vessels. I am from Brest bound to Bangor. If you come down to the cabin, I'll show you my papers," replied the captain, holding back his anger.

Would the Frenchman find a flaw in the papers? Mrs. Deborah wondered as the two men went below, followed by Mr. Bliss, his long face grim and his tight lips moving in some soundless hymn. Even the children felt the suspense. They looked at the French sailors below them in the open boat; they looked at the great frigate riding the waves at ease a little beyond them. Far, far off some sail, no larger than the wing of a moth miller, hurried along the horizon as though in flight. But here was the *Fair American*, crippled and helpless, at the mercy of the whim of this awkward young officer, who could send them off with a prize crew, if

111

he wished, and ruin Captain Patterson by selling ship and cargo.

If only the foremast had not broken, they would not have been so easily caught, Andrew thought. He looked like his father at that moment, his shoulders squared; his young chin thrust out a little; his gray eyes, usually so thoughtful, shining now with indignation.

Still no sound came from the cabin. What could they be doing to take so long? Mrs. Deborah held her hands tight-pressed together to keep them quiet.

Ah, footsteps!

The sailors sprang to attention. Mrs. Deborah turned even whiter than before. The French officer appeared with Captain Patterson, talking stiffly.

"Thank you, captain," he was saying. "I find your papers in order. May I wish you a good voyage?"

It was all right then. A little sigh came from Mrs. Deborah's lips. It may be that Pierre unconsciously exclaimed in French. If he did, he could not remember it afterward; but the officer swung toward him with a sudden sharp glance.

"Who is this boy you have with you, captain?" he demanded dryly, looking Pierre up and down.

Mrs. Deborah swept forward, facing the officer with a strained smile.

112

"*Peter's the oldest*"

"Il est à moi," she answered, *"le plus aîné!"*

It was the first French she had ever spoken, except with the children. Why she should have spoken in French at all she could never say. "And Aunt Debby telling a fib!" thought Sally. "He is mine, the oldest!" Well, if Aunt Debby could fib, so could Sally!

She came forward now, smiling her most engaging smile, and slipped her arm about Pierre's neck.

"Peter's the oldest," she said, "and then comes Andrew, and I'm the youngest. My name's Sally." She left Pierre, who had not moved, and came up to the Frenchman and curtsied.

"Have you any little girls at home, sir?"

His hard young face changed, looking down at her.

"Yes," he said, "but little Victoire is still a baby. She cannot even walk yet. But she has brown eyes like yours."

"I'll send her a present!" cried Sally, and ran off.

She was back while her clear voice seemed still in the air, with Eunice, her doll, in her arms.

She gave it to the Frenchman.

"Remember," she warned him, "put Eunice in your berth and let her sleep. She is not a good sailor."

A twinkle came to the overserious eyes of the young man.

"I will remember," he replied with great politeness. "Vic-

114

toire will join me in a thousand thanks for your kindness."

He bowed to Mrs. Deborah, to the children, and called to one of his sailors, who appeared over the side to take the doll carefully down into the boat. Then he bowed and shook hands with Captain Patterson.

"You are to be congratulated on your charming family," he said. His eye rested again a little sardonically on Pierre, with his foreign look, his thin young body too large for Andrew's clothes, his bare feet.

Then, with a salute, he was gone.

They stood at the rail watching the boat pull away. The officer was standing at the stern, and he had Eunice under one arm.

As Sally waved, he took off his hat with a sudden boyish gesture and waved it vigorously.

"Sally, you've been guilty of bribery!" exclaimed Captain Patterson. "After you'd gone into action, he couldn't make trouble without seeming like a brute—even to himself. But you've lost Eunice."

"I'd rather lose Eunice than Pierre," said Sally stoutly. But she did not look at her uncle, for she was watching the last glimpse of Eunice's pink dress—only a little spot of color now under a distant dark blue arm.

A horse would tire,
But I, I do not tire.
A stag would turn,
But I still keep my course.
A bird must rest,
And ashes follow fire,
But I excel
Flame, bird, or deer, or horse.

Only the wind
Do I require for ration,
Only the waves
Beneath my forefoot curled.
Eager I run
From nation unto nation
And seek my harbor
Halfway round the world.

XIII

THE BIRD FLIES FREE

It was America that rose before them in islands and cliff-edged shore, in blue rounded hills patterned with cloud shadows. The gulls that veered about them were American gulls; the wind that came to them had the smell of American spruce, and was warmed by long passing over the land.

"We'll be at Winterport tomorrow, and then they'll send word to Uncle Joseph to come for us!" cried Sally, jumping up and down. "Dinah! Dinah! You'll be home before you know it!"

Pierre stood absorbed in this new landscape that seemed incredibly savage to him. Here he was to spend his life, a stranger. The shores were wooded. Only occasionally could he make out the square of a field; only once did he see a white spire. The green lonely land stretched before him, almost like another sea. What did people do in this wilderness? It was not like anything he had known.

"I'm glad it isn't," he thought. "The people here are kinder. Here there are no rich or poor, I believe. Everywhere there is land, as far as one may travel. They have never come to the end of it yet."

The thought of such great distances frightened him a little.

"But they say Boston is a city," he comforted himself. "There I shall find my Uncle René and my Aunt Thérèse. Captain Patterson knew of them very well. He says that Uncle René is a merchant and much respected." He paused, and his mind went back to the old order of things.

"What would Mother have thought to have had her brother a merchant! But here it is considered no disgrace. Perhaps I, too, shall be a merchant."

He took a deep excited breath. There was no telling what he might become. Nothing was closed to him now—all roads were open. In the old days he had supposed he would have to be a courtier like his father, whose whole life must be lived in the hope that the King might notice him, if only to say "Good morning."

Now he was free to be anything. He felt the pleasure he had begun to feel on the Breton moors, but deeper, more assured. Pierre laid his hand down on the rail, hard, glad to feel the impact of the smooth wood under his palm. He was standing at the bow just aft of the mended bowsprit. Sally and Andrew were in the cabin, packing their little horsehide trunks. He was alone with America.

Jon passed him with a grin, did something to a sail, and disappeared. The *Fair American* was bowling along, in a fresh breeze, passing now and then a fishing boat or coastwise sloop, bobbing in the sparkle of the waves. She seemed to approach the land eager but skittish, like a well-bred horse in a pasture, that comes toward its master, but now trots off to his left, now to his right, before finally it lets itself be touched and haltered.

Now the boy could see, through the islands, the mouth of a great river which he knew must be the Penobscot. They were entering it. How far it seemed to reach up into the land! Tomorrow, the sailors said, they should be at the little town of Winterport, where Mrs. Deborah and Sally and Andrew would go ashore.

Pierre heard Sally's quick step behind him—and there she stood, leaning beside him at the rail.

"How good it smells!" she said. "And, coming down, Andrew and I counted seven deer drinking along one of the creeks. I wish, Pierre, you were coming to the farm too."

119

"You have all been so good to me," answered the boy warmly. "Especially you, Sally. You nodded to me from those steps in Brest. Do you remember? I have a little present I should like you to take as a keepsake."

Pierre drew out of his pocket the package Jean had put in his hand at parting. Sally helped him open it and then exclaimed over the pair of earrings that lay there, shaped like baskets of gold, with flowers whose petals were rose-colored diamonds.

"How beautiful!" she said, just touching one with the tip of her finger.

"They are for you," Pierre went on proudly.

"Oh, I can't take them!" cried Sally, drawing back.

Pierre was hurt.

"Yet you gave the officer your doll," he said, a little sullenly. "Why won't you take my present?"

Sally tried to think out why it was different.

"Eunice was all mine," she explained at last. "But these were once your mother's, weren't they? You must keep them, Pierre, for her sake."

He folded the earrings back in their cloth and put them again into his pocket. His fine gift had been refused. All his life he had been accustomed to give favors, rather than to receive them, and the new lesson was not easy.

"Pierre," Sally was saying at his elbow, "Pierre, may I borrow them for today? Please, Pierre. I'll be very careful. But I should so love to show them to Aunt Debby and everyone. They will have seen nothing like them, ever."

Pierre's face brightened again as he handed her the jewels. Even this temporary acceptance took the sting out of her refusal, and gave him the pleasure of putting the earrings into her hands. As she ran off with them to find Aunt Debby, something deep in his heart acknowledged that he was glad not to be parted forever from this last token of his old life.

All afternoon the weather held fine; but toward evening a coldness came into the air, followed by the whiteness of fog, pursuing them from the sea. The fog bank stood up like a wall in the east, advancing faster than the *Fair American* could sail. First Pierre noticed that the sunlight grew paler, then the shores seemed farther off, and at last he could not see even the tops of the masts above him. Dripping, cold, and blinding, the fog enveloped them.

Sally, like an angry little wraith, appeared at Pierre's side.

"Oh, drat!" she exclaimed, stamping with vexation. "Now we'll have to anchor somewhere, and goodness only knows *when* we'll get to Winterport!"

Pierre looked at her anxiously.

121

"Don't cry, Sally," he muttered.

Sally threw back her head.

"I'm *not* crying," she protested. "It's just this nasty wet old fog on my cheeks!"

A sob choked her.

"Anyhow, I'm crying for anger, not for sorrow!" she insisted, head in the air, tears raining down her cheeks unheeded.

"Are you so eager to be ashore?" Pierre asked, a little sadly.

Sally looked at him with widening eyes, then, with one of her sudden changes, threw her arms about his neck.

"No, I'm not," she said. "How silly I am! Just because I expected a thing is no reason to think I want it so much! Maybe I'll be at the farm all the rest of my life, and then I'll be wishing I'd been longer on board ship."

They anchored soon after in a cove. The children knew a farm must be near, for they could hear cowbells and the sudden barking of a dog; but all they could see was a glimpse of a big pine tree now and then, that would appear, like a ghost out of the fog, for a few minutes and then fade slowly from sight again.

After supper Captain Patterson rowed ashore with Mrs. Deborah, who said she didn't mind dabbling her skirts so long as she could step on Maine soil once more. The children played games of hide and seek all over the deck, which had become as mysterious as the heart of a cloud. They could pass within a few feet of one another and see nothing, unless a sudden giggle betrayed the hider. Dave Coffin, who was lame from a fall he had once had from the shrouds, got out his accordion and played for them, and afterward Black Tom sang negro songs that made the children shiver with their strangeness and wildness.

It seemed no time before the boat was hailing them; and there were Mrs. Deborah, with a blueberry pie in a basket, and Captain Patterson, looking huge as he loomed up over the rail.

"I was right about this being Morang's Cove," he told the children. "Mr. Morang's driving to Winterport in the morning, and he thinks he can get word up to your Uncle Joseph at the farm to come down to meet you the first clear day. You're delayed here instead of at Winterport, Sally, so I shall have you all with me for at least one extra day."

"A treat! A treat!" cried Mrs. Debby gaily. "Mrs. Morang sent you all a treat!"

Pierre ran for plates and forks, and the mate joined them; and soon they were all eating blueberry pie, though by now

123

the light was so dim that they could scarcely see their own hands.

"This is what America tastes like," thought Pierre. "It is dark and fragrant and wild."

Next day the fog never lifted; but the hours passed swiftly, with something of the same chill magic of the evening before. The children played a game they called "Guess." They guessed what sound they would hear next—a gull's cry, the crowing of a cock, the turn of wheels along an unseen road, or the rustle of Mrs. Debby's skirts. Then they would guess what they would see next out of the fog. When at last they wearied of games, they pretended they were Indians and surrounded the galley and scalped Black Tom and carried off a plateful of sugar buns. The day had a curious sweetness, because they knew it was likely to be their last all together—at least for a long, long time.

During the evening the wind swung into the northwest, and suddenly the stars began to appear and disappear among the tattered and fleeing fringes of the fog. The air felt drier and kinder. By earliest dawn the *Fair American* was tacking up the river again, past lowlands and bluffs almost like mountains. The whole landscape was incredibly bright and clear. The water sparkled, the pines along the shores shone darkly, the gulls seemed like floating snowflakes against a sky that blinded one with its blue.

"We live way up the river, don't we, Andy?" Sally explained to Pierre. "Yes, it's just as beautiful as this, isn't it, Andy?"

"It's better," said Andrew in his grave way. "The farm is way up over the river, Pierre, near the Indian tree with the pictures on the bark, which Sally and I found. You must come to see it someday. Someday, not in summer, so that I'll be there too. Summers I'll be mostly sailing with my father, I expect."

"I'll come," said Pierre. When, he did not know, nor how he would come. But someday he would surely come to see them again and thank them. He would be really Pierre L'Étranger, then—an American too, as they were.

About noon the *Fair American* eased into a berth along the river wharf at Winterport, among the two or three sloops already there. Captain Patterson called a greeting across to the captain of the *Active* of Newport, the sailors exchanged witticisms from deck to deck; but Mrs. Deborah, Andy, and Sally had eyes only for the short determined-looking woman and the two men who stood smiling and waving to them from the shore.

"Uncle Joseph!" screamed Sally. "Aunt Nannie! Uncle Eben!"

Aunt Nannie shook her head vigorously and laid her finger to her lip in an attempt at reproving Sally for her boisterousness, but her eyes were shining. Uncle Joseph was smiling, a quiet warm smile of satisfaction.

"Welcome home, you wanderers!" roared fat Uncle Eben.

Just then the gangplank was run out, and Sally skimmed over it and leaped into Uncle Joseph's waiting arms, laughing and crying. An indignant meow from the basket on her elbow showed that Dinah disapproved of the jolting she had had; but Sally was beyond paying any attention, and was off into Aunt Nannie's arms next, and then into Uncle Eben's, where she was swung high into the air, basket and all.

Mrs. Deborah and Andrew followed, almost as eager as Sally. There was an exchange of news.

"Sister Esther has had a fine little boy, and they've named him Joseph after Brother Joseph."

"The farm's done well."

"Brindle lost the tip of her horn, Aunt Nannie."

"Brother Joseph, we were caught by a most fearful gale, but I had such confidence in my husband I felt no uneasiness."

"How is Peacock, Uncle Eben?"

Then Captain Patterson came ashore, bringing Pierre with him, with little Turk at his heels.

"This is Pierre, who escaped with us from the Revolution-

Swung high into the air, basket and all.

ists," Sally explained. "And this is my Uncle Joseph, and Aunt Nannie, and this is Uncle Eben who makes us laugh so much."

"I hope you're coming back with us to the farm, boy," said Aunt Nannie kindly. "We can easily put a pallet for you in the unfinished chamber."

Pierre thanked her gravely, but he was on his way to join his uncle in Boston.

"Then I'll be going ashore with you, my lad," said Uncle Eben. "You see, there's a young lady near Boston who won't marry anyone but me, she says; and as Brother Patterson has his vessel here ready, I think I must oblige her."

"Are you getting married too?" asked Sally. First Aunt Esther and then Aunt Debby and now Uncle Eben! She felt sure Uncle Joseph and Aunt Nannie would stay single. But someday she supposed she would marry too—marry Andrew if he wanted her, and she had no doubts about that.

"Tell dear Eliza she is much too good for a lazy old bear like you, Eben," cried Aunt Debby, in one of her flashes of mischief.

Uncle Joseph drew out his heavy watch and looked at it.

"I don't like to hurry a parting," he said, "but, Brother Patterson, I believe you are not unloading here and plan to go out with the tide. And if we are to reach Five Bushel

128

Farm by daylight, we must start. Jehoshaphat Mountain is here with an oxcart to take the boxes and anything Debby has brought back with her."

"But the rose tree goes home in my lap!" declared Aunt Debby. "I've nursed it for ten weeks, and it's still blooming."

Leave-taking was hard, even now when it was not for long. After the cargo was disposed of, Captain Patterson planned to spend a month at Five Bushel Farm. Uncle Eben would come back with him, bringing the new Aunt Eliza. But the summer was drawing to a close, the adventure was over. They would never all be voyaging again on the *Fair American*, at least not with Pierre. The sailors lined up along the rail to say good-by. There was Nantucket Bob, hauling Brindle ashore. He had told the children so many stories in the lee of the longboat. And there was Jon, fair and kindly, and Black Tom, grinning and waving good-by with a dishcloth; there was big Dan Forrest, whom they had saved and who in return had saved them, and the lame boy who played the accordion, and all the rest.

"Good-by, good-by! Thank you! Good-by!" called Mrs. Deborah and Andrew and Sally.

Peacock, prancing at the hollow sound of his hoofs on the wharf, had been led near by Uncle Joseph. Captain Patterson and Uncle Eben helped the ladies into the carriage. Aunt

Nannie and Aunt Debby, with her rose, sat in the back seat, while the children perched in front, beside Uncle Joseph. Pierre stood near Captain Patterson, feeling rather forlorn.

Just then the carpenter hurried up, with Dick in the cage he had once made.

"You've forgotten your bird, ma'am," he said, pulling at his forelock and grinning.

"So I had," admitted Mrs. Deborah. "Thank you for remembering." Her eye fell on the boy on the wharf.

"Pierre," she said, "will you take care of Dick for me? He ought to be yours; you caught him, and he's a French bird, you know."

"May I do anything I like with him?" Pierre asked eagerly, taking the cage.

"Surely," she said. Then she added, "You'll set him free?"

He looked at her, and nodded, his eyes bright.

"In Boston," he said.

"In Boston," thought Mrs. Deborah, "they'll both be free." And at the word she seemed to feel a sudden rush of air past her face, and see the sun rising bright and far away.

Upturned faces

Surely, even the ship knows
It was for this—for this home-coming—
She fought against the waves, and set her sails
For the least capful of the breeze;
It was for this she groaned and struggled on
In the grip of the storm;
It was for this
She sped before the wind;
Always, always, somewhere ahead,
  somewhere beyond the waves,
There lay the landfall,
Docks,
And upturned faces.